7|20

1. Five

2. Things

3. About

4. Ava

5. Andrews

FIVE THINGS

ABOUT AVA ANDREWS

MARGARET DILLOWAY

BALZER + BRAY

An Imprint of HarperCollins*Publishers*

Balzer + Bray is an imprint of HarperCollins Publishers.

Five Things About Ava Andrews
Copyright © 2020 by Margaret Dilloway
All rights reserved. Printed in the United States of America.
No part of this book may be used or reproduced in any manner whatsoever
without written permission except in the case of brief quotations embodied
in critical articles and reviews. For information address HarperCollins
Children's Books, a division of HarperCollins Publishers, 195 Broadway,
New York, NY 10007.
www.harpercollinschildrens.com

Library of Congress Control Number: 2019957962
ISBN 978-0-06-280349-8

Typography by Jessie Gang
20 21 22 23 24   PC/LSCH   10 9 8 7 6 5 4 3 2 1
❖
First Edition

This one's for Kaiya.

"LISTEN. SAY 'YES.' LIVE IN THE MOMENT. MAKE SURE YOU PLAY WITH PEOPLE WHO HAVE YOUR BACK. MAKE BIG CHOICES EARLY AND OFTEN."

—Amy Poehler, Harvard University Commencement Address, May 26, 2011

CHAPTER 1

"Tell me something you've never told anyone before."

Zelia leans toward me. The lamplight makes her brown eyes glint with amber and caramel. On my end, I shift to the right a little so the sun stops hitting my screen.

We're lying on our stomachs, looking at each other through our phones. Zelia pets her purring long-haired black cat, Willy Wonka. Tufts of his fur fly off and drift through the air like dandelion puffs, landing on the hardwood floor of her bedroom. He stretches, the long fur between his toes swooping like ribbons. His toes are the funniest cat toes I've ever seen. Behind Zelia is her unmade bed, the familiar blue comforter thrown to one side.

"Something about me? That'll be hard. I think you know more about me than I do." I shift my elbows on the carpet. Zelia and I have been best friends since first grade, and now we're in sixth. If there's a secret I'm keeping from her, I don't know what it is. I make a quick list. Anxiety. Writing. My heart. Art. Everything that makes me crazy afraid or wildly happy—Zelia knows it all. "You first." I wonder if the same is true for her—do I know all her secrets?

"Okay. I have one." She flutters her lashes against her freckled cheeks. "Um. You're not going to like it."

My pulse pauses. What is it? Does she secretly dislike me? Does she have an identity I don't know about? "Spit it out."

She lowers her eyes. "I had a crush on Luke last year."

"Ewww!" I almost hit the phone away, I'm so surprised. And grossed out. "You had a crush on my brother?" He's in eighth grade and, granted, a lot of girls crush on him—but that's only because they don't know how bad his personal hygiene is.

She claps a hand over her mouth, giggling. "Just for like two seconds."

I'm glad she kept that a secret. It definitely seems like something I didn't need to know. I glare in pretend anger and shake my pointer finger at her. "It's a good thing you moved to the other side of the country, young lady."

"And then I saw him chewing with his mouth open one time when we had mac and cheese, and yeah. My crush got crushed forever." Zelia's laughing now, tears

2

dripping out of the corners of her eyes, and I laugh, too, my breath fogging up the screen.

I remember something then. One of the only things I've kept from her. "This is pretty random. But remember when we split up the jar of Jelly Bellies?"

She nods. "What about it?"

We'd gotten one of those huge containers from the bulk store and tried to divide all the flavors evenly. I'd taken all the light orange ones because Zelia hates them. "I don't really like the cantaloupe-flavored ones at all."

"You don't?" Her eyes widen. "But you said . . ."

"I never said I liked them. I said I'd *take* them." I shrug as best I can, with both elbows on my floor.

"Oh, Ava." Zelia rolls onto her back and Willy Wonka sits on top of her chest. "You should have told me you didn't like them, either. I could have given them to my mom. I feel bad!"

I reach out toward the screen, pretending to pet Willy Wonka. He stares at my finger like it's some weird kind of bug and takes a half-hearted swat at it. "Next time, I'll try to tell you." I know I won't say anything like that because I want Zelia to be happy. Even if it means I don't get what I want. Isn't that what friends do? "I wish you were here. Sixth grade is horrible without you."

"You don't know that." Zelia pets Willy Wonka harder, making more fur fly. "You've never been in sixth grade with me. Maybe it would be *worse* if I were there."

3

"Doubtful." I laugh. "At least at your new school, you get to be the cool kid from California. Here I'm just plain old Ava."

"It's only the second week. And you're still alive."

"You sound like my parents." They like to point out obvious things, too. It would be annoying, but now I expect it.

"I like your parents." Zelia turns over onto her back and grins at me upside down.

"Zelia, bedtime!" Zelia's mom calls from a room I can't see.

"You heard the boss lady." Zelia rolls back over and makes Willy Wonka wave at me. "Night night!"

"Night night!" I wave back and hit end. The clock appears. It's only seven o'clock here and I've got two and a half hours of nothingness before bedtime.

Zelia moved to Maine two months ago, but it feels like she's been gone for two decades. Luke says that's impossible since I've only been alive for one decade plus one year, but I know what I feel like.

In middle school, Zelia and I were going to start an anime club and cosplay at Comic-Con. I was going to write a whole book for her and she was going to help me get it published.

We were going to be the popular kids, the ones who got invited to all the parties. I mean, I actually don't know anyone who has parties, but I'm pretty sure they exist.

"Just think, Ava," Zelia had told me. "At a new school we don't have to be who we were in elementary."

"But most of the kids are the same," I'd pointed out.

"It doesn't matter. New school, new life." Zelia always points out things I don't think of.

I look at the clock again—only five minutes have passed. I could go watch television with my parents, or even go outside because the sun hasn't set yet. Instead, I act like I'm on the opposite coast with Zelia. I change into my pajamas and climb into bed with my journal. At least we're still close, I tell myself. Even though we're thousands of miles apart, she and I are in the exact same position, doing exactly the same thing.

School just started and I'm already behind. I bend my head over my work, ignoring the clang and chatter coming in through the open windows. I'm using my lunch period to work on the English homework that's due right after the bell. Mostly so I don't have to eat alone.

Unfortunately, this is the worst English essay in the history of English essays. I'm so going to fail. My stomach feels like it's got a thousand itchy ants in it, and my limbs go numb. Fight or flight or freeze. I'm freezing. I shouldn't be.

It was the most boring of times, and then it still was the most boring of times.

There's no sound but the rhythmic tapping of the

keyboard as the librarian checks in books or whatever librarians do. I stare up at the bulletin board that's covered with club and activity flyers. Chess. Leadership. Engineering. Builder's Club. Soccer. Football. Improv.

Improv was Zelia's thing. She taught me a couple games from it, like Words of Wisdom, where we each said random words until it made a sentence. Those were fun to do with her where nobody could see, but I'd never do them onstage, in front of people.

Thinking of her while I'm alone hurts like getting lemon juice on a paper cut. My parents keep telling me to pick an activity because they say it'll be good for me. I can't imagine walking into a club and awkwardly hanging out by myself. Well, actually I can—that's why I don't want to go.

Besides, trying new things without Zelia feels disloyal, somehow. Like secretly watching an episode of a series alone, when you're supposed to be watching it with your family on Friday nights.

I put my head down on my table, inhale and exhale deeply, noticing what's nice about my surroundings, like Mr. Matt, my therapist, tells me to do. I love how a library smells, even a library where a bunch of stinky teenagers have been hanging out. The sunlight streams in through the waving leaves of the trees outside the windows. My back somehow fits snugly into this ancient plastic chair, which they probably bought when Dad was a student here.

It's my favorite place at school, probably because it's the quietest. The hallways are deafening with shrieking kids. The lunch arbor hurts my ears. Even the classrooms are usually noisy. We always have to do group table work, and the kids at my tables talk over me. Like the person with the biggest voice automatically wins.

The library kind of helps me recharge. And the librarian has the most perfect name that a librarian has ever had—Ms. Bookstein. She told me once that she'd planned to not change her name if she ever got married. Then she met Mr. Bookstein. "His name was probably thirty-three percent of the reason I liked him," she said.

I'd thought that was funny. My mom kept her last name, Tanaka, when she married my dad. I can't imagine ever getting married, but if I did, I don't think I'd change mine, either. I like my name, Ava Andrews.

My thoughts have gone off topic again. I sit up straight and hold my pencil above the paper. I have to write this, not think about last names. We read an excerpt from *A Tale of Two Cities* and now we have to write like Charles Dickens. I'm afraid the teacher, Mr. Sukow, is going to think I'm making fun of it.

What I wrote sounds like something Mom would say. In fact, I'm pretty sure Mom put it into my head. "Dickens?" my mother had said when she saw the assignment. "You should just write *snooze* over the whole paper." But Mom thinks anything without a spaceship in it is yawn-worthy.

Dad just grumped that Mr. Sukow should have had us read all of *A Tale of Two Cities* instead of a few pages. Even though that probably would take me all three years of middle school. "When I was your age, I read *Moby Dick*," he said. From how he talks, when Dad was my age he read college-level books and invented fire.

I grab my writing journal. My real journal, with my story for Zelia in it. I'd much rather work on that. "Ava?" Ms. Bookstein's hand rests on my shoulder, and I jerk my head up. "How's it going?"

My stomach clenches again and I think about faking a stomachache to get out of fifth-period English. But no. I did that last week so I could skip a group talk about grammar. Dad isn't going to fall for it another time.

I shrug and show Ms. Bookstein my Dickens line. "I'm having trouble with this." My voice sounds weak and hesitant, even in this quiet room. Although I'm only talking to gentle Ms. Bookstein, I want to yell with frustration, but these emotions won't come out through my mouth. I don't know why—it's like I'm Dad's record player, with a stuck needle that keeps playing the same part over and over again.

Ms. Bookstein chuckles, her short fingernail skimming the words. "This is good, Ava."

"Really?" I look up at her. Ms. Bookstein has been so nice to me this year, letting me come into the library whenever I want. Never nagging me to go talk to kids.

She lets me be. I shouldn't need her permission or whatever to write, or think I'm good, but I like it anyway.

"You'd better hurry. Only ten minutes left." She points at the clock.

I put pencil to paper.

CHAPTER 2

In English class, we hand in the homework, then do some grammar-type stuff on our own. I sit in the aisle closest to the door. It's one of the accommodations in my 504 medical plan for school, which lists the things I do to manage my anxiety and my heart condition. The ability to leave makes me feel less nervous about having to sit in a class. My first choice would be the back row, but Mom says I only want that so I can hide. Which is true.

Mr. Sukow is reading my purple journal with *AVA ANDREWS* on it in green gel glitter pen, his reading glasses perched on his little ski-jump nose, and I can't sit still. He frowns, he smiles, he shakes his head, and each movement makes my heart jump. Mr. Sukow is a very expressive reader. I'm pretty sure I'm going to get a zero, and then my parents will ground me. My brothers will make fun of me. It'll go on some kind of permanent record and I'll be stuck in sixth grade for two years. I'll be the only twenty-year-old to graduate high school.

This is what Mr. Matt calls *catastrophic thinking*. I interrupt the imagination train like he said to. I ask myself, *Is that really true?* No, my parents probably are not going to ground me, I admit. The only time they grounded anyone is when my oldest brother, Hudson, snuck out in the middle of the night to go to a party. This isn't nearly that bad.

My fourteen-year-old brother, Luke, might make fun of me—but he'd also make fun of me just for thinking any of this could be true.

I force some deep breaths in and out, wishing like crazy that Zelia was sitting in front of me. She always calmed me down. With her in the lead, all I had to do was hold on, like Zelia was the racehorse and I was the little cart she pulled.

Without Zelia, it's impossible to make friends. Dad says I just need to talk to people. "If you sit there saying nothing, people assume you want to be left alone," he's told me. But it's easy for Dad. He runs a business where it's literally his job to teach kids to have manners and be social butterflies. Every kid but me. I'm probably Dad's greatest disappointment, a fact I try not to think about because of the molasses string of sadness it pulls out of me.

The boy behind me pokes my spine. Ty. "Do you have a pencil I could borrow?" he whispers.

I do, in fact, have an extra pencil. I can even give him

my special blue sparkly one. But my whole body stiffens at the thought of talking to him, as though Ty just poked me with a pocketknife and not his finger. Yay, anxiety. I try to force my voice to talk, but all that comes out is a little squeak.

I guess he expects me to actually say yes or no, though, because he lets out a disgusted little noise. "Never mind. I'll ask someone else."

Wait, I want to say, but he's already borrowed one. I sag down toward the earth. Too little, too late. I return to my work, apologizing silently to Ty.

After a little while, Mr. Sukow dings the bell on his desk, and everyone goes still. "Let's read some of these out loud." He shuffles through the journals. If only I had an invisibility cloak right now. Instead, I hold my breath and try to become one with my desk.

Ms. Bookstein said it was good, I remind myself. *You won a writing award in fifth grade. Zelia loves your stories.* There's nothing to worry about.

But that was elementary school, and Zelia's not here.

I can feel my heart thumping in every far-off part of my body. My fingertips, my toes, my scalp.

Mr. Sukow waves the journal and gives me a questioning look—*May I?* he mouths. Alarms go off in my head. Does he want me to read it or is he going to? If I were a robot, there'd be smoke coming out of my ears. My systems go into overdrive, like my brain thinks I'm in the Serengeti and just spotted a lion about to pounce on me.

I think I'm going to die.

I try to deep-breathe, but my chest hurts, my heart going wonky. The stress of it overwhelms me and my bladder both. I should read it. Participation's part of my grade. I nod at Mr. Sukow but also raise my hand for the bathroom pass, an index finger pointed to the ceiling, the signal my teachers agreed on that I can use, no matter what else is going on in class. It's my get-out-of-jail card.

Mr. Sukow nods and I go up to the front and grab the yardstick that we use as our bathroom pass, accidentally meeting Ty's glare. His eyes remind me of the *National Geographic* photo I saw of Arctic ice on a cloudy day— blue green but kind of dark. He wrinkles his freckled nose at me. I turn and shuffle-run out of there, faster than I've ever gone during the PE mile, as if Mr. Sukow is going to haul me back in like an escaping fish.

"How come she gets to leave whenever she wants?" I hear Ty complaining as the door closes, but I don't care. My lungs were like plastic bags stuck together and now they're filling with air. Is it my heart or my anxiety? It has to be my anxiety, but thinking about my heart makes me more anxious. I put my hands on my knees and gulp in oxygen, then go down the hall to the bathroom, taking as long as I dare, not wanting to hear whatever's going on in my classroom.

CHAPTER 3

When I get back, everyone's working at their desks. I sit down. I got out of reading my work but now I have to worry about reading it tomorrow. I'm going to think about it all night.

After class, Mr. Sukow stops me. "Ava, I read your story to the class while you were out."

A surge of heat overtakes me. I had nodded at him— and nods mean yes, so I don't know why I'm surprised that Mr. Sukow can't read my mind. I look past him, at a ding on the doorjamb. I imagine the whole class snickering with glee, all of them saying, *That Ava is so stupid, thinking her story's good. My little brother wrote a better one when he scratched his crayon on the wall.*

It's also part of my 504 that I not be forced to stand up in front of groups unless I've had warning, so I can prepare. My heart thumpity-thumps once more, and I automatically put my hand over the scar below my left collarbone, feeling the hard outline of the ICD pacemaker there. The ICD stands for implantable cardioverter defibrillator—it's like what you stick on people when their heart stops, to shock them. Anxiety makes my heart weird, on top of the genetic condition I've got, noncompaction cardiomyopathy. Basically it's spongy heart tissue that can make your heart beat wrong. This could either make it stop beating or make it get bigger, and big hearts don't work as well—they get kind of floppy.

I must look shocked because Mr. Sukow continues. "I saw you nod—so is that okay? I didn't want to stress you out by asking you to read."

I touch the ding on the door. "I guess it's okay." It's not super okay, but what else am I supposed to say? Besides, he can't go back in time and not read it. I look at my black Vans.

"It's very funny. We all loved it." He pats me on the shoulder. "I hope you're comfortable enough to read your own work one day."

Wait, he thought it was good? And he's not annoyed with me for leaving? My brain's too confused to answer. The class loved it? Mr. Sukow is probably exaggerating. When sixth graders don't make fun of something, that means it's all right, or they didn't want to make him mad. Not that they love it.

I seriously doubt that I'll ever be relaxed enough to read my own work aloud. If Zelia were here, she would have done it for me. She would be talking for me now, saying, "Don't you worry about Ava. She's fine how she is. She doesn't need to stand up in front of people if she doesn't want to."

I sit with that thought for a moment, until another comes to me.

The thing is, I do really want to. Sometimes.

I want to share grade-A work. I want to be able to talk to people. I don't want to pretend the library is my first choice at lunch. But when I have to do these things, it's like my body literally freezes up, as if I'm a rabbit hiding from a vicious dog.

"Ava?" Mr. Sukow asks. "Are you all right?"

I nod automatically. It doesn't matter. This is who I am, how I was born. And I just have to accept that.

After school, my backpack's hurting my shoulders and my spine, and I have to stop before I leave campus and try to rearrange it all. It feels like I'm carrying twenty soup cans around.

If Zelia were here, she'd carry my backpack for me. She's a good friend like that. When we walk in groups, she always turned around to make sure I didn't fall behind. To wait up.

I think about calling my grandfather or step-grandmother for a ride. I sit down against a wall and pull out my phone, then think better of it. Jīchan only lives two blocks away. The doctor says walking helps my heart.

I'll never be a triathlete, but I should try to be healthy.

Then a girl from English class jogs up and I cringe as if she's a bee buzzing toward me. Cecily—I recognize her as one of Zelia's improv friends. I've never talked to her, but I've seen her at Zelia's shows. "Hey," she says a little breathlessly. Her dark hair is cut really short, and I've heard some kids tell her she looks like a boy, but obviously she doesn't care. I think that's pretty cool. "Your story was really good."

Thanks, I want to say, but my stupid throat clenches in on itself like a fist, so I half turn away from her and nod instead. I don't know why my body reacts like that, but it does.

She doesn't say anything else, so I don't say anything else. We search each other's faces for a few seconds. Her skin's kind of a honey bronze, which makes her green eyes stand out. Mine's probably turning the color of a stop sign. "I love your hair," I say instead of anything important or clever, but to my relief she smiles.

"You're Zelia's friend, right?"

I nod.

She shifts her backpack to her other shoulder. "I haven't texted with her since she left. How's she doing?"

"Good." I think of Zelia, and the plans we made to be the best we could be at our new middle school. "She likes the autumn in Maine. It's already a lot colder than here. She sent me a package of fall leaves." We don't have those in San Diego—only a few trees turn red and gold, and usually not until December.

Cecily clears her throat. "Say. I have to miss English tomorrow for a doctor's appointment." She smiles. "Could I text you for the assignment?"

My face still feels hot. "S-sure," I stammer. I tell her my number, and Cecily texts me hers.

A minivan honks, and Cecily waves at someone. "That's my ride. I gotta go."

"Okay," I say. "You go ahead." What a weird thing to say. Cecily doesn't need my permission. She runs off.

I look at my phone. *Cecily. Text me whenever.*

A mix of relief and excitement fills me. Cecily thinks I'm a good writer. Maybe she thinks I'm kind of cool. Or at least okay. Or at least wouldn't mind talking to me again.

It'd be nice to have a friend, instead of this carved-out jack-o'-lantern sensation that Zelia left. Sitting alone at lunch. Playing video games alone every weekend.

I could do stuff with Cecily. A movie reel plays in my head of me and Cecily skipping through fields. Maybe she likes to draw, too, or watch the same kind of movies, or even just hang out like Zelia and I did.

Or maybe she just needs the English assignment.

No, brain, I tell myself. *Don't be such a hater.*

I walk to my grandparents' house, forgetting how much my backpack had been bothering me.

CHAPTER 4

That evening, Dad's in the kitchen making spaghetti and salad. I sit at the island, watching. He's wearing his casual outfit: pressed khakis and a tucked-in polo shirt. His sandy-brown hair is neatly combed. Mom says Dad looks like a handsome '80s movie villain, and Mom is into villains—her favorite Disney character is Captain Hook, after all. I'm just glad he doesn't try to dress like a hipster.

Dad owns a Cotillion program for sixth graders. It's a social skills course where kids learn manners, basic ballroom dance moves, how to eat at a fancily set table, how to shake hands, how to make small talk, and a bunch of other boring stuff. His father ran it before him, and Dad says it's a proud Andrews tradition. He does it all over the county, with classes meeting in the evenings.

Dad likes to make Cotillion into a big deal. He sends the students an invitation through the mail—not even email—and everyone has to dress up. The worst part is that you have to both talk to and dance with strangers. Hold hands with strange boys—gross. I have brothers. I know where those hands have been.

It's a completely awful thing to make kids do. I mean, both Luke and Hudson said it was the single most terrible experience of their lives. But Mom and Dad say it's a "rite of passage" for sixth graders. At least sixth graders around here.

My stomach gurgles painfully anyway, and a tidal wave of exhaustion hits my chest. I don't want to go to Cotillion.

"Hungry? Have some carrot sticks." Dad pushes a plate toward me. "We have to leave by six to set up."

I put my face down on the counter, pressing my cheek onto the cold granite. "My tummy hurts. I'm tired. I just want to go to bed."

"Faker." Luke bounds into the kitchen, still dressed in his dirty soccer uniform. At least he took off his cleats and socks. He opens the fridge and drains the milk carton of the last drops, then lets out a window-rattling belch.

"Cotillion obviously didn't work on him. Why should I have to go?" I glare at my tattletale brother. He never believes me about my anxiety and thinks I just try to get out of stuff because I'm lazy.

Luke grins, grabbing a handful of carrot sticks and sticking them all into his mouth at once, like the man in *Guinness World Records* who smokes dozens of cigarettes at the same time.

"He'll be thankful one day. You all will be." Dad rolls his eyes. "Why haven't you changed, Luke?"

"I was doing homework." Luke says this like it's a valid reason to not change out of gross, grass-stained clothes.

"You smell like a sick duck who lives in an algae-covered pond." I wrinkle my nose.

Dad chuckles. "That's quite the image."

"Yeah?" Luke counters. "How do you even know what a sick duck smells like?"

I shrug, satisfied with what I said. "Like you."

"If you're well enough to make jokes, Ava, you're well enough for Cotillion." Dad stirs the pot of pasta. "Eat some bread—your stomach's just nervous and churning up acid. That will settle it." He hands me a piece of French bread he's making into a garlic loaf.

"Fine." I take a bite. Cotillion in my family is like going to the dentist—there's no choice.

There's a knock at the side door, and then my grandfather sticks his face in. I jump up at the sight of his tanned, friendly smile. "Jīchan!" I run over and hug him.

He smells comfortingly of grass and pine needles. He pats my head. "Hey, Ava. Don't mind me. Just returning the jigsaw I borrowed." He waves at my dad. "I put it in the shed. Thanks."

Because Jīchan and my step-grandma live so close,

they're always popping in. We borrow stuff from each other all the time. Dad says between the two of them they have enough tools to open a Home Depot.

My phone buzzes. FaceTime from Zelia. I scurry to the living room, slipping my earbuds in. I'd called her after school, but she didn't answer, so I'd texted her what Cecily said to me.

"See you later!" I hear Jīchan call out.

"Hey," I say as her beaming, lightly freckled face appears on the screen. She's lying on her bed, petting Willy Wonka. I can hear his purr clearly. Next to her is a water bottle covered with stickers that say *San Diego* and *Navigando Point* and *San Diego Improv*. "How are you today?"

She gives me a thumbs-up, and I thumbs-up her back, exactly like we're together in person.

When Zelia and I met in first grade, she saved me. I was sitting cross-legged on the playground when three boys came around, bouncing one of those hard brown balls. "What's your name?" the lead boy demanded.

Why do you want to know? I wanted to ask. I didn't like how they were looking at me. Like they were the bosses. My heart beat faster and my body got hot. I shook my head.

"Why are you sitting here?" another boy asked. I said nothing, just crumbled a leaf.

"If you don't talk, I'm going to bounce this ball on

your head." The boy held it high.

I couldn't make my body move. I knew I should shout or run, but my whole mind stopped working. As if by not feeling anything, I could hide.

Then, out of nowhere, Zelia appeared like a raging lioness, her caramel-chocolate-colored hair flying around her. She was the tallest girl in the class then. She's still taller than me now. "Leave her alone!" She grabbed the ball out of the boy's hands. "What has she ever done to you? Get out of here before I tell." She hurled the ball at the boy so hard he caught it in his stomach with an *oof*.

She helped me up, and it seemed as if some of her energy transferred to me. "Are you okay?" Zelia asked. "Don't worry. I won't let anybody hurt you."

And so I trusted her.

I can talk with people I know and trust, no problem. It's just that there are very few of those people around.

"I saw Cecily today," I tell her. "She says hi. She's in my English class."

"Ohhhhh," Zelia breathes. "Cecily is the best. She's so good at improv. Ahh, that makes me miss it!" Zelia's fast-talking and loud, and I relax, knowing I won't have to say much.

"Yeah," I say because I don't have anything else.

Zelia leans forward so all I can see are the whites of her eyes. "They don't even have improv here, except for the one at my mom's college! Which obviously I can't do."

Sympathy snaps like a rubber band inside me. I know how much Zelia loved being in that improv class. Some kids have sports, but Zelia's had this since she was eight, taking classes at the theater. "That's horrible. I'm sorry."

"Yeah. I don't know. It doesn't seem like anyone here likes the same stuff I do." She changes the subject. "How was lunch? Did you eat with anyone?" She takes a sip of water.

"You sound like my mom," I tease. But truthfully, Zelia knows me too well. Ava and Zelia were the Best Friends from A to Z. It didn't matter if the teacher started turns at either end of the alphabet because one of us always got to go first, and then helped the other.

I don't want to tell her I have lunch alone and then go into the library, so instead I tell her about my essay, and then she makes me read it to her, and she laughs so hard that water spurts out of her mouth and nose onto Willy Wonka, who gives a startled *Meowr!* and runs away, and this makes me fall over laughing, too.

It's at times like these I can almost forget Zelia's not here.

CHAPTER 5

Everyone else is already at the table when Dad calls me to dinner. Luke and Hudson had set it tonight. I hope mostly Hudson because I really don't trust the way Luke washes his hands.

"Hello, milady." Hudson pushes his floppy brown hair out of his face. "Milk or water?"

"Milk—I'll get it myself." Hudson enjoys doing things for me, but I don't want him feeling like my servant. He's seventeen, six years older than me, but somehow we're closer than Luke and I are. I'm Hudson's beloved younger sister, but Luke's supremely annoying little sister. Hudson was ten when I had heart surgery, old enough to be worried about me. While I was healing, he hung out with me every day, reading me stories or just letting me snuggle.

Unfortunately, I hardly ever see Hudson these days. Junior year's the hardest, plus he drives himself to ballet rehearsal most days. Hudson's been in dance since he was four.

"Don't worry, Ava. I'm having milk, too." Hudson glides into the kitchen, looking like he's about to jump into one of his ballet moves. Which is how Hudson always walks. People tell me my brothers are cute. A lot of Mom's Japanese features—high cheekbones, a slim straight nose—have come out in them. I look more like Dad. An '80s movie villain, female version. Plus I don't wear khakis. I think my nose is too big for my face and my cheekbones are more like moon pies stuck on the sides of it, but Mom says I'll grow into myself. Which is like a thing moms are required by law to say.

"Need any help with your math?" Mom beams at me. Her short black hair sticks up all over the place, and she's wearing a plaid shirt with a Darth Vader T-shirt underneath. Mom's a bit of a Star Wars nut. She wanted to give us all weird names—I was supposed to be Padmé—but the only one she got away with was the normal-sounding Luke. "Dad didn't even realize what I was doing," she chortles every time she tells the story. She's an aerospace engineer for a defense firm and works a lot of hours. Dad does most of the housework stuff.

"I finished my math homework." I actually don't know whether it's correct, but I do know that Mom gets super frustrated when she checks it. Mom has a real frenemy relationship with how they teach algebra these days.

She's super good at math, but the way she does it isn't the way the teachers want us to do it. So she'll end up emailing the teacher, *Listen here. I have a master's in mechanical engineering and this makes no sense, and you'd better straighten up before I come down there and have a math-off with you.* Or something like that.

I'd rather avoid math with Mom.

We eat silently because my brothers and mom are too busy chewing to say anything. "Thank you for making dinner, hon-bun." Mom kisses Dad. My parents are like oil and vinegar, they're so different from each other. But as Dad says, "You need both to make a good salad dressing." He should print *that* on a T-shirt.

"You're welcome." Dad smiles at her like she just told him he won the Nobel Prize. My parents are kind of hopelessly in love for such an old couple. "Boys, do the dishes."

Hudson nods, already finished, and clears away his plate. "Anyone need anything from the kitchen?" He points at me. "Want seconds?"

"I'm good, thanks." We thumbs-up each other.

Luke grumbles. "Why doesn't Ava have to do dishes?"

"Cotillion," I say sweetly, glad for the first time that I'm going.

"I had an email from Zelia's mom today." Mom breaks off a piece of garlic bread. "She says you're invited to visit next summer." She and Dad exchange a glance.

I almost jump out of my chair as an excited jolt surges through me. Immediately I picture it. Me and Zelia watching anime and drawing like we did until she left. Swimming at the lake or catching lobsters or fighting bears or whatever people do in Maine. "Does that mean I can go?"

Mom purses her lips. "I'm not sure."

I deflate like a beach ball thrown into a rosebush. "You never let me do anything."

"You have a hard time asking the teacher for a bathroom pass," Dad points out. It's why we came up with the finger method. "What happens if you get lost in an airport?"

"They have accompanied flights for minors," Mom says. "Besides, she might mature this year." They both look at me.

"Doubtful." Luke covers his mouth with his hand and belches. Like the hand makes it better. *"Excus-eh moi."*

Dad shoots him a stern look. "Maybe if she does a good job at Cotillion. Learns how to look people in the eye. Talk to strangers. All that good stuff."

"That's not hard at Cotillion," Luke scoffs. "I got through that thing without saying more than five words. *Do you want to dance?"*

Dad draws his bushy eyebrows together and clears his throat. Luke's pushing it. Nobody insults Mr. Andrews's Cotillion to his face and gets away with it.

Luke backs off. "I'll go start the dishes." He clears his plate and disappears.

Mom sighs. "We'll see." She cocks her head at me, her mysteriously shy third child, like she examines troublesome engines, to figure out what's causing the weird malfunction.

Except Mom can't fix me.

CHAPTER 6

Cotillion is held in a large auditorium at a middle school—not my middle school, but a different one about fifteen minutes north of us—that's packed with boys and girls wearing suits and dresses. I'm wearing my favorite dressy navy pants and a royal-blue blouse. Mom says I look sophisticated. Dad's father always made the girls wear dresses, but Dad changed things when he took over.

In the old days, Dad and my grandfather owned a big space in a shopping center full of industrial warehouses, in between a printer's shop and an auto body place, that was pretty close to our house. I used to like to go there because some artists rented the smaller warehouses for their studios, and on hot days they'd have their big metal doors rolled up so you could see what they were working on. Once, a woodworker gave me a little wooden car. But that whole center got torn down to put up stores and some fancy apartments, and Dad could never find a new spot anywhere near our neighborhood.

So now Dad rents middle school auditoriums, which he has to schedule a year in advance. He tells me to sit on the girls' side and then goes off to do his thing. Dad is really in his element. His dad, my grandpa Andrews, ran this business before he died. I don't want to take it over and I doubt either of my brothers will want to, either, though Dad says it's a community staple that should be kept going. He's got boxes of thank-you letters from adults, saying that the skills they learned here helped them become successful.

Because Dad's been doing this forever, you'd think he'd do the same thing over and over, but he always makes little tweaks. For example, when he was younger, he didn't have to teach anyone about cell phone etiquette. (Which is to PUT IT AWAY WHILE YOU'RE WITH REAL PEOPLE.)

Obviously I'm the first kid to arrive, so I sit alone in a folding chair. Maybe I should help unfold chairs or something, but I'm afraid I'll mess up. Say the wrong thing. Squish somebody's finger in the chair hinge. I'm nervous the same way I was before I had to get my tonsils out three years ago and I googled the risks of anesthesia.

It's a good thing I was too young to google when I got the ICD pacemaker. I was four, and I don't remember any of it. Now the device sends the doctor reports, and I go in for a checkup once a year. I try not to think about it too much because it'll set off an anxiety attack for sure, and that isn't great for hearts. Anxiety can actually make the heart muscle beat irregularly in the first place. In fact, Dr. White says that some research points to anxiety as the thing that sets off a disease like mine.

But now I'm thinking about it, so I turn my attention to Dad and his assistants getting everything ready. Older teens volunteer for school community service hours, plus there are some parents who set out bowls of punch and Dixie Cups.

"Thanks for the help," one of the older girls says sarcastically to me as she and another girl carry a batch of folding chairs across the auditorium. "I didn't think Mr. Andrews would have a spoiled kid," she whispers.

I sit on my hands, my chin on my chest. My head turns hot. Great. Now I've brought shame onto Dad as well as me. Because I'm quiet, sometimes people think I'm a snob. Zelia was the one who always told everyone, "Ava's really cool. She's just shy."

But what am I supposed to say without Zelia here? *Hey, I'm cool, I'm just shy.* I don't think so.

I want to cry. I pick at a hangnail instead.

Finally, the kids start coming in. Girls float into the auditorium wearing a variety of fancy dresses and boys come in wearing dress pants and shoes that look too big. Which they probably are. I know for a fact that a lot of these boys will grow like three inches before Cotillion is over in March, and their parents probably bought their shoes too big like my parents did with my brothers. By the end, the shoes will fit. The parents sit behind the kids on both sides and anywhere they can find a spot.

Nobody talks to me. A lot of these kids don't go to my school, though some do. Three girls I know—at least, I know of them, but we're not friends—sit down near me. Kiley, a super-popular redhead; Becca, who has shiny black hair; and Cherine, who has long, intricate braids.

I was in Scouts with them for a little while in elementary school. That's one activity Mom had me do that Zelia didn't. Every meeting, they talked over me even if I managed to raise my hand. And they didn't talk to me then, either. Eventually I stopped wanting to go.

They're the kind of girls who will probably grow up to be in Congress or the president or something. People like me—the quiet thinkers—never get to be the leaders. Even if we have good ideas, we can't get anyone to listen.

They're also the kind of people who don't notice girls like me. Not because they're mean, but because I'm sort of invisible to them. Like I'm a chair.

Maybe I could actually be a good spy.

As I'm considering changing my future career choice from writer to CIA agent, Dad—Mr. Andrews—goes into the middle of the room with his microphone and starts talking about all the useful stuff we'll learn this year. "Manners are like a sink. You don't notice how it functions until something goes wrong. Manners keep society flowing smoothly," he says, and then gives the same lecture about courtesy that I've heard every day since I was born.

I think of all the times I've tried to do group stuff. The soccer games where I just stood there. The softball innings where I couldn't bring myself to swing the bat in case I struck out (spoiler: *not* swinging gets you out, too). The ballet class where everyone else pliéd and I tucked myself into a corner, crying until Dad came to collect me.

Afterward, every single time, I wished and wished I could have done something. I wanted to kick the soccer ball into the goal net. I wanted to swing the bat like I did during practice. I wanted to plié like I did when I practiced alone in my room. I just froze every time.

Cotillion is no different.

When Dad tells the boys to get up and walk across the room to the girls, asking them to dance, I'm the last one to stand. "Don't run," he instructs the boys. "And don't try to get to a specific girl. Ask the first one you see to dance. And, girls, don't try to get a different boy to ask you instead."

I fidget as the swarm of boys gets closer, like a slow wave heading toward a beach. They look like they'd rather be anywhere else on the planet than here, asking girls to dance. I recognize some of them from school.

I nudge myself to the side, trying to wait. If I hang back long enough, I'll be a "leftover" girl because there are always more girls than boys signed up, so a few always have to sit out. That means I'll only have to dance twice instead of three times.

A short boy with a runny nose gets to me, though. "Dance?" he says to my feet.

Thanks for the enthusiasm, I almost say, but instead I nod, and we awkwardly grab clammy hands as Dad uses one of the mom volunteers to teach us the box step. For me, it's right foot back, left foot back and to the left. The lead, the boy, does the mirror image. I've danced this all my life with Dad or Luke or Hudson, so I end up kind of dragging this boy along. He looks possibly more miserable than I feel, which is really something. He also needs a tissue.

"Now you're going to make conversation with your partner," Dad says over the loudspeakers. "Small talk. Ask where they're from, what they like to eat, what their favorite sports team is."

The music starts. "Moon River," a super-old version sung by some guy named Andy Williams. Dad is obsessed with this song. He says it's perfect for teaching beginners. I say it's kind of cheesy and have begged him a hundred times to get some new music, but Dad's way too stubborn. I also know it's exactly two minutes and forty-four seconds long. I can survive that long. Maybe.

"What's your name?" I ask.

"Harold."

I can almost do this part in my sleep because Dad's made me so many times. "Nice to meet you, Harold. I'm Ava." I comb my mind for another standard question. "What's your favorite sports team?"

"I don't like sports," he says.

I feel my spine melt into a slouch. Dad says you're not supposed to be negative like that. He told me to say, "I'm not really into sports, but here's what I really like." Always offer something.

We dance-shuffle in a small circle for a while. We've both got sweaty palms. Harold lets go of my hand to wipe his own on his pants. Dad always says not to do that, but he hasn't told this class yet.

I try to smile at him but my face feels like a creepy doll's, all strange and fake, and he doesn't smile back.

Finally the boy mumbles, "What school do you go to?"

I can't stand it. If I don't say something interesting, both of us will implode. Last night, Dad and I were watching *Masterpiece* and imitating British accents, pretending we were going to see the queen. "I go to Blogwarts," I blurt out, as if I'm talking to Dad and not a stranger. "My magic wasn't good enough for Hogwarts." Then I blush, mortified that I actually said it. Maybe he'll laugh and play along like Dad would.

Harold looks at me like I'm a weirdo, probably because I suddenly, I don't know, *grew an English accent*, and I flush all over again. "Is that a Harry Potter joke?"

"Yeah," I say faintly. I'm such an idiot. Thankfully the dance ends and I return to my chair and put my head in my hands, turning away when the next song starts. I'm going to be a leftover this time if it kills me. Dad sees and I know he's thinking about saying something, but he doesn't. I'll thank him later. Right now I sit here alone, waiting for the end.

CHAPTER 7

After all the kids leave, the other volunteers and Dad put the chairs away. I'm not looking forward to getting into Dad's car. A lecture is brewing. I can sense it like Jīchan can sense rain coming in his arthritic knee.

At last, after we're buckled and he's pulled out of the parking lot, Dad clears his throat.

"I noticed you sat out most of the dances. I think we should talk about it."

"Okay." By "we" he means him. *He* needs to talk to *me*.

He begins. I already know exactly what he'll say, so it's easy to tune him out. *Participate. You're not allowed to just sit there. You have to learn how to do these things. If you don't talk, people think you're unfriendly, and I know that's not what you want.* I stare out the window at the lights whizzing around us. If I squint at the yellow lines, they look like one long one while we're moving.

But then, before we even reach the freeway, Dad's

words sputter to a halt like a broken engine. He sighs. "Maybe I'm being too hard on you."

Wait, what? I look at him. Dad looks . . . resigned. He gives me a tiny smile. "Remember what we talked about with Mr. Matt?"

Mr. Matt told Dad that lecturing me didn't really work. He can't Dad-talk me out of anxiety. Instead, Mr. Matt told him to let me lead. Be encouraging, not over-bearing.

"I know it's hard for you, Ava. Impossible, even. So if you want to stay home, I'll understand."

My stomach jumps, and it takes me a few moments to realize I'm not at all happy about this like I thought I'd be. I feel like I did when I got caught hiding Luke's favorite teddy bear years ago. Ashamed.

Dad's giving up on me?

This is not a Dad-like thing to do. Dad doesn't always completely understand my anxiety, but he never gives up on me. He's like Zelia in that way.

I always thought that if Dad decided *not* to lecture, I'd be relieved. I'm not. It makes me even more anxious, like the time my third-grade teacher gave up on making me do the multiplication tables because she thought I couldn't do it, when I was really just scared of messing up.

Maybe I really will never be able to do what I want.

"But." I wipe my clammy hands on my dress pants.

"What about our deal? I do this and go visit Zelia?"

He shrugs. "The choice is yours. You can't just go to Cotillion and not participate. But if you don't go, then you won't get to visit Zelia." Dad puts on the turn signal for the freeway entrance. "You can think about it." Then he accelerates to get up to the right speed, throwing me back a little in my seat.

Dad's given me an out. But the out might be worse than the in. I chew on my fingernail, an old bad habit, and stop myself. Whatever I do to solve my problems, I think I'm going to have to do on my own.

Two days later, I wake up to a text from Cecily.

Anything happen in English?

No, I reply. She should have texted last night so she could do the homework, if we had any. I was waiting all evening for it. Then, because I'm feeling salty and I'm always saltier over text, I add, *But if you really wanted to know, you should've asked yesterday.*

Then I worry that sounds too mean, so I send a smiley face.

She doesn't respond.

I chew my nail. Was I too sarcastic?

But then she sends a laughing face, and I realize it's only been about a minute. *Yeah, I know. I was totally being lazy. See you later.*

I smile. *See you.*

* * *

During lunch, I go to the library and shelve books. A lot of people might think this is boring, but I like it. I like pushing the cart around to the different aisles. Most of all, it's cool to see what other people are reading. I've found a lot of books I wouldn't have known about as I was returning them to their proper spots. Today I've put aside three. I'm trying to limit myself.

Today I've got a Chicken Soup for the Soul, hoping to be inspired. A *Ten Things All Successful Students Do.* And a new fantasy series.

I put away a couple of books, wondering what Zelia's doing right now. If she were here, obviously I wouldn't be in the library. We'd be out in the lunch arbor, me listening as Zelia told a story, the other kids laughing until milk and juice came running out of their noses. I'd be so proud to be her friend. I'd be included.

Suddenly Cecily pops out from behind the stacks. "Hi, Ava!"

"Sheesh." I grab my chest. Luckily my heart's okay at being surprised. "You scared me!"

"Oh my gosh, I'm so sorry." She touches my arm. "Zelia told me about your thing." She gestures at my torso.

"I'm fine." I wave her off, embarrassed. She stops in front of me, her Alexander "Cat"-milton shirt taking up my whole view. It has a cartoon cat posing in

1700s clothes. "I like your shirt," I say, mostly to change the subject. I bet everyone tells her that. I should have thought of something more clever.

"Thanks! I actually have a question for you." She leans on the cart and puts her face in front of mine and blinks her clear green eyes. "Are you at all interested in improv?"

My heart thuds extra hard. "Improv?" I whisper, as if Cecily just walked up and asked me to commit a crime with her. "*Me?* No." I pick up a Percy Jackson from the shelf. This is the wrong section for it. I put it back on the cart for now and start wheeling to the fiction section.

"Listen." Cecily trots after me. "You probably think you're too quiet to do it, but when I heard your story, I knew you'd be good. It sounded just like you were talking in character."

I make a face.

"And it's fun. I promise!" She gets in front of me again. "Didn't you play pretend when you were little? Like with action figures and stuffed animals?"

I flash back to playing with Zelia, and a warm feeling surges over me. "Sure."

"It's exactly like that. We just play."

She makes it sound so easy, but I've seen it. I know it's not. The performers get suggestions from the audience, then act out scenes or games based on that. So they might ask the audience for "favorite dessert" and get "cupcake," and then there will be a scene about two best friends who are having a birthday party where an alien might show up. I never get how they do it. How can people make up all that stuff on the spot? I mean, I can if I'm writing. But not while *talking*. That's a hundred percent different.

I shake my head. "That's not my thing." The stage is Zelia's thing. I'm the friend clapping for her.

"Besides, we only have five people. So Miss Gwen— that's our coach—"

"I know who Miss Gwen is." She was Zelia's coach, too.

"Someone dropped out. Miss Gwen told us to find at least one more person or she'll have to cancel the class. They have a six-person minimum." Cecily leans on the bookshelf.

I shelve the Percy Jackson. "You should ask somebody else."

"Please. Just one class." Cecily bats her eyes at me.

There's zero chance I'm getting up in front of strangers and making up things out loud. I actually have a better probability of growing wings myself.

I try to remember what Dad told me to do in this social situation—if I don't want to do something, I should refuse instead of pretending I want to and then flaking later, which is a million times ruder. Should I say that my family is against improv? That won't fly. "Um, thank

43

you for the invitation, thank you for thinking of me, but I'm not sure that's for me, I mean I really need to ask my parents because I saw that it does cost some money." I spit this out in one breath, horrified with myself. Why didn't I refuse? And why did I talk so much?

That's a problem I have. When I can finally get my mouth going, sometimes it goes too much. Like a dam bursting and causing a flood that wipes out an entire village.

But Cecily nods as if she didn't notice my verbal brain fart. "Well, just come on Saturday if they say yes."

I nod. They're going to say no. Even if I only ask them in my imagination.

Cecily jerks her head toward a table. "I'm going to finish my homework. I'll see you in English."

"See you." I nod at her, then begin pushing the cart back toward the front desk. "No way am I doing that," I mutter.

"Doing what?" Ms. Bookstein asks from her computer.

"She wants me to do improv." I say it as though Cecily asked me to rob a bank.

I expect Ms. Bookstein to say, *You should do it!* But instead she kind of laughs. "Oh my. I totally understand you not wanting to try. Not your cup of tea at all."

My spine stiffens. "Why?" This reminds me of the time last summer Luke sneered that there was no way I could ever beat him at Mario Kart. It made me so mad that I played after bedtime every night until I could do it.

"It'd be like asking a fish to ride a bicycle, wouldn't it?" Ms. Bookstein smiles, and I'm sure she means to be kind, but what it really means is she's given up on me. Like Dad. Nobody thinks I can do anything. "We all have our strengths."

My eyes sting and I stare hard at the book cart. I remember all the different activities I've tried. All those sports I was terrible at. And Cotillion, which isn't even a sport—I can't do that, either.

Every single activity is a memory of how I messed up and what a loser I am. I know Mr. Matt says that's not how I should think of myself, so I correct it: *I* acted *like a loser. I am not a loser.*

Then I remember what Dad said about how I need to show them I can do stuff.

I love the library, but is this really the only thing I can do if I've never even tried other stuff? I remember Mr. Matt telling me how my anxiety becomes a big problem if it prevents me from doing the things I want to do.

I think about Zelia. About disappointing both of us if I can't go out there next summer. I would be letting her down big-time. And how cool would it be to fly across the country by myself?

Being in improv would *have* to prove I've got myself under control. It would show everyone that I can do what I want.

45

And Zelia always talked about how improv helped her talk to people. What if doing improv helps me do Cotillion? If I do Cotillion, then I will for sure get to visit her.

Words pop out before I realize my mouth's moving. "Actually, I think I will do improv."

"Oh." Ms. Bookstein's eyes widen. "Okay. That's great, Ava."

"You'll do it?" Cecily pops up from her table. "Yay!"

Too late to take it back. My throat dry, I nod. "I will." I don't want Maine to be like a sports incident. Something I wished I'd done and then thought about forever. If improv helps me get to visit Zelia, then it'll be worth it.

CHAPTER 8

That night, while Mom and Dad are watching *Jeopardy!*, I appear in front of them with a page ripped out of my notebook. "Here." I thrust the paper at them, then go sit in the armchair and put the pillow over my face so I don't have to watch them read it.

I wrote them a note explaining why I want to go to improv. I know they're going to say, *Oh my gosh, you in improv?* Just like Ms. Bookstein. It seems like such a weird thing for Ava Andrews to want to do.

Dear Mom and Dad,
  This may come as a surprise to you, but I want to do improv. Cecily (you may remember her from Zelia's shows, though her hair's short now) invited me.
  As you know, I'm having some trouble in Cotillion. I believe this may help. I really want

to go visit Zelia. I hope you will allow me to
participate.

    Sincerely yours,
    Ava Andrews

Mom giggles.

I lift the pillow. "What?"

"That's an excellently written note." Dad nods. "Very formal." I smile. Obviously I wrote it like that for him.

"So Cecily invited you? That's great!" Mom claps her hands. "A new friend! I knew it would happen!" She whips out her phone and signs me up almost before she finishes her sentence.

Mom always gets ahead of herself.

My phone buzzes. I get a text from my grandparents saying, *Improv! Good for you, Ava.*

"Mom!" I almost throw the phone away from myself. Next thing you know, they'll want to watch me perform. "Did you text Nana Linda and Jīchan already?"

"Of course!" Mom pulls me into a hug. "Progress is progress."

"You're so corny," I say, but as I put my face on her shoulder, I smile to myself. Usually my parents and grandparents focus on me because they're worried. To have them pay attention because of something good feels way better.

* * *

I take a deep breath straight from my gut and in through my nose, like Mr. Matt says to do, hold it for four counts, and blow it out slowly from my mouth. I'm gathering up my courage. It's Saturday morning and Dad's parking the car at Navegando Point, a little shopping center down by the San Diego harbor. *Navegando* means "sailing" in Spanish. There's a really old, wooden-horse carousel and a duck pond, and the buildings are all old-fashioned, like a sea shantytown. Some are brown and some are painted in brighter colors.

My parents like it because it doesn't cost very much to have fun here. You just have to buy one thing to get your parking validated. When my family goes, we always get ice-cream cones or cupcakes and sit on the wall by the sidewalk, watching tourists and trying to guess where they're from. We stare out at the boats floating by in the bay, the ocean beyond, with white clouds skipping along the deep blue mirror of the water, or watch street performers playing one-man-band instruments or juggling.

Every time we come here, we stop by a plaque that reads *Punta de los Marineros*, or Sailors' Point. In the 1700s a bunch of sailors from Spanish ships who were surveying the port died of scurvy and are for-real buried underneath this shopping center.

"I can't help thinking about the fact we are walking over a cemetery," I say to Dad as we get out of the car.

"It's the same thing with Old Town," Dad says. That's

another touristy area of our city. "They actually have grave markers on the sidewalks."

I shudder a little bit. When we've gone to visit my grandmother's burial plot in the cemetery, my parents made sure to tell us it was disrespectful to walk over the graves or run around. But people are doing that all the time in these places. I wonder if in three hundred years people will be shopping on top of our graves, too.

"It is morbid," Dad says, "but a lot of history is like that."

"I guess." I follow him out of the parking lot and we take the winding path through the shops, past the duck pond, and reach the theater. Outside a sign reads *San Diego Improv* in glittery cursive. A couple takes a selfie in front of it.

Time for class. My stomach gurgles like I'm going to barf. My hands go icy.

Dad clears his throat. I've been so lost in my head, I forgot he was next to me. "You want me to walk you in?"

No, I want you to drive me back home, I almost say. "No thanks." The only thing worse than being nervous about this is having my dad come in.

"I'll be back in two hours." Dad sticks his hands in his pockets. "You have your phone. Call or text if you need anything."

I feel like I'm going to the first day of preschool. I want to tell him not to go. Before I can answer him, Cecily pops out and grabs my hand. "Yay, Ava's here!"

She takes my hand and pulls me inside, closing the door behind us.

I follow her through a dark little lobby, past a snack stand and register, and past some heavy black curtains that have been pulled to one side.

I've been here before to watch Zelia, but it's always been dark inside. Today the lights are all on, so I can see everything. It's about as big as a classroom, but the walls and ceiling are painted black. Lights hang above us, pointing at a small, short stage. There are rows of movable chairs in front of that, where a few kids sit. I try not to look at them in case they're sneering at me, like Ty.

Miss Gwen stands on the stage, marking a clipboard. She's young and has long curly blond hair that's wonderfully messy in the way that an alpaca's hair is messy. Not only does she teach at the theater and at schools across San Diego, she's also a performer—she's on a couple of their professional, grown-up improv teams. Zelia took me to see a few shows and Miss Gwen was amazing.

Miss Gwen gives me such a warm smile that I can't help but smile back. "I've seen you before." She points at me. "You're Zelia's friend Ava. Tell her we miss her."

"I will," I respond. I'm surprised I talked. I'm also surprised, in a good way, that she knows my name. It feels like being recognized by a celebrity or a popular kid or something.

We form a circle. Again my intestines seem to coil and

strike like a cobra is inside me. I wonder if I can watch for a while. Tell Miss Gwen that I need time to adjust.

Then Cecily surprises me by pulling me into the center of the circle. "Everyone, this is Ava." She picks up my right hand as if I'm a doll and makes me wave. Normally I'd be freaking out, but the way she does it makes me giggle. "Don't scare her away."

"Hi, Ava!" the kids all say at once, as if they're excited I'm here. They start introducing themselves. I try to nod and smile and repeat each name like Dad taught me, but it's too hard because my brain just wants me to run, not learn. I hide behind Cecily.

"I've seen you before. You're finally taking a class!" a boy with dark red hair says. He looks at me in a way that reminds me of Hudson, when he's teaching me how to beat a really hard boss in a video game. "I'll help you." Ryan—his name pops into my head from Zelia's shows. He's a sixth grader at our school, but we don't have any classes together.

"We'll all help you," a tall girl with medium-length curly brown hair and olive skin says. She points at herself. "I'm Babel." Pronounced *buh-bell*. "Like the Tower of Babel." She looks as old as a high schooler—I definitely would have thought she was old enough to drive—so I figure she's in eighth grade. She's dressed cooler than the rest of us, like she bought all her clothes at the thrift store and created a style that nobody else has. She's wearing a suede vest with fringe, a graphic T-shirt, and some vintage jeans.

I wonder if she could take me shopping.

"Improv's really not that hard." The blond boy with the freckles, Jonathan, steps in. He's wearing a gingham shirt with a red bow tie and has thick-rimmed glasses like the kind celebrities wear. "That is, certainly sometimes it's complicated. And there are about a hundred things to remember at any given time. But it's not *hard*."

"Nothing's hard for Jonathan, though," Cecily says. "He takes high school math."

"What I mean is, if you break down improv into its simplest components, it is not difficult, just like math," Jonathan continues. "You start with the most basic elements. One plus one is two. Two plus two. Etcetera. You learn more, and keep building. And eventually you reach calculus."

I wrinkle my forehead. "Improv is like math?" I wonder if my dad's gone yet. I can still leave.

"You're not making it seem that great, Jonathan," Cecily says.

"We don't bite," a short boy with a booming voice says. I recognize him from school, too. "Unless you want us to." He snaps his teeth in the air, and the other kids mimic him, and then they all howl like wolves.

"Enough!" Miss Gwen says above the roar in her high, clear voice, and they go quiet. She steers me into the circle between the short kid and Cecily. Then she points at Ryan. "Zip!"

Ryan points at the short kid, Chad. "Zap!"

Short Chad points at blond Jonathan. That's how I'm going to have to remember them for a minute. If I put an adjective with their name it's easier. "Zop!"

My heart beats a million times per second, but the game's easy to figure out and I don't have a chance to worry about it. People take turns saying *Zip! Zap! Zop!* when they get pointed at. That's it.

Babel points at me. "Zip!" I say, and am super happy when Miss Gwen gives me a little nod. Like I'm extremely smart and talented and she knew it all along.

The game continues and we go faster and faster, and when someone messes up, we join hands and jump into the air and yell, "Hooray!"

"We celebrate our mistakes here," Miss Gwen says. "These warm-ups are designed to make you mess up. You're *supposed* to mess up." She delivers this like my preschool teacher telling me it was okay to dip my fingers into the paint.

A place where you can make mistakes and nothing bad happens? I don't believe it. I try to follow along with the exercises as best I can, worrying the whole time something tragic will happen if I make a mistake. Somehow I manage not to. Probably because I'm being super quiet.

Next we do an exercise where we pair up with a partner and give each other pretend gifts. "Make the gift the worst thing you can think of," Miss Gwen says. "But nothing offensive. Then the receiver will say, 'thank you, I always wanted a *blank*' and say why they like it so much."

We split into partners, which means whoever's on our left. Chad's mine. I'm not sure I get it completely. "Don't worry," Chad says, as if reading it on my face. "It's easy. Give me a gift first and I'll show you."

"Go!" Miss Gwen claps.

I stare at Chad for a moment, frozen. I can't think of anything! This is too hard.

Chad nods like he understands I'm stuck, then turns his body like he's picking up something behind him. He pretends to hand me an object. "Here's a bag of toenail clippings!"

Gross! No! I almost say, but I'm supposed to be grateful. Chad waits for me. After a few seconds, I choke out "Thank you. I always wanted a . . . bag of toenail clippings." I wrinkle my nose, and Chad and I both giggle. "I'm going to . . . uh . . ." What can I use them for? "They're great for fertilizing a garden!"

Both of us dissolve into laughter. "This is all about the *yes, and*," Miss Gwen says. "This is the most important part of improv and, I think, one of the best. Your partner gives you something, and it might not be what you wanted. You say *yes* and add to it, make it positive. Make it something you *want*." Miss Gwen beams at us. "That's why you're saying thank you plus a reason for why you wanted this item."

Oh. That makes sense. I remember all of the times I've automatically said no to things. It took me forever to try sushi, because I didn't think I wanted it. When I finally ate it, I ended up liking it a lot. Which is probably good since my family wants to eat it at least once a month. What if I'd said *yes, and* to that? I would have saved myself a few years of struggling with it.

It's my turn now. This time I say the first thing that pops into my head. "Here's a gift . . . a broken plate that's in a hundred pieces!" I pretend to hand him a bunch of little shards.

"Thank you!" Chad exclaims. "I've always wanted a broken plate. I'm going to put this into a piñata instead of candy!"

We giggle again. "You see," Miss Gwen says, "when you're doing a scene with someone, they might tell you something you don't expect. You might think they made a mistake. But you turn that into something really funny and wonderful."

Chad pats my back. "Good job!"

"Uh, you too!" I say. This isn't so bad. The kids are really nice.

* * *

After another short exercise, Miss Gwen has us sit in the audience chairs. "Close your eyes," she says. "We're doing our walk-through. Imagine Navegando Point. What do you see? Who are the people you see?"

I shut my lids. This class isn't as scary as I'd thought it'd be. Imagining stuff quietly is definitely something I'm good at. I could do this all day.

I picture Navegando Point. We haven't been here in a while. We used to visit a lot more, when the bookstore was open. It was a really cool space with a loft where you could get coffee and all kinds of bookish gifts. But that closed a couple years ago.

Last time my family came here, we saw a juggler on stilts, throwing knives up in the air for tourists. Lots of those were around, taking photos, arguing about where to eat lunch. A teenager in black, looking bored despite the knives flying through the air and playing with the small hoop earring stuck through his bottom lip.

"Pick a person," Miss Gwen says. I already did.

"Eyes open," Miss Gwen says. "Now we're going to do our monologues. I want you to come out as the person you chose, and talk like you think that person would."

My heart skips. I thought this was a sit-down thing, and suddenly I have to be onstage all alone? Cecily volunteers first, standing off to the side and then walking all hunched over, in a quivery elderly woman's voice. "Oh, would you look at that? Water! I've never seen so much!" Cecily toddles around with an imaginary camera, taking photos.

She continues for another minute until Miss Gwen stops her, and we all applaud. I still hold the character in my head, and my heart beats even faster. Not because I'm scared or because I want to run away.

Because I want to try.

To my surprise, I want to get up there and let out this thing that's building up in me. To have fun like Cecily's having.

Ryan leaps up next, and he does a super-high-energy man who yells everything, really physical, stomping around the stage. "Gotta get me some of that shucky darn dang cotton candy!" We giggle.

After Ryan finishes, my hand creeps up from my lap. Just the fingers, really, but Miss Gwen sees. "Go ahead, Ava," she says, stopping Chad, who's already up. Chad gives me an *after you* gesture with his arms and a friendly smile, so I get up, knees shaking, and Cecily sticks her hand up for a high five that gives me just enough courage to step onto the stage.

We celebrate our mistakes here.

I'm going to swing the bat this time.

"Yeah, Ava!" Chad bellows.

"Do it, Ava!" Ryan calls. "You got this!"

They all clap for me and it reminds me of a baseball team hollering for a player that's at bat. And that kind of pushes me forward like Cecily's high five.

I don't have time to argue with myself. I don't even try. I step out, moving like the character, dragging my feet like Luke does when he's doing something he doesn't want to do.

I only know who I am, not what I'm going to say. I slump over and play with the imaginary earring in my lip. I'm the Bored Emo Teenager, dressed all in black, annoyed with the entire world. What Hudson calls a "Sad Boy."

I let out a long, loud sigh. "My parents are so bogus, making me come to San Diego for spring break. They say it's America's Finest City. But ice-cream cones cost seven dollars, and a seagull pooped on mine. It's just one annoying thing after another." Snorts come out of the audience.

I move around the stage, my head to one side like the teenager I saw. "You know what my ideal spring break is? Sitting alone in my room. Which I painted black." A big laugh pushes me along. "Listening to the saddest songs ever, as loud as possible. And writing poetry. I do all this in the dark. Lights out. That's the kind of spring break I want to have." I shake my head. "They want me to be like my brother Johnny. Just because Johnny's student body president and plays basketball and everybody loves him doesn't mean I should be like him. You know?"

"Awww," a few people murmur.

The hair on my neck and arms stands up. I'm talking about my brothers, I realize. Though my parents have never said it to my face, I know my parents wish that I was more like them. Wish that I could just chill out like they do.

I mean, I kind of wish that, too.

"But I'm not them. I'm me." I shrug.

The class startles me by bursting into applause. It's not the kind of soft claps people do just to be polite—they liked it.

Am I supposed to bow? Now all my feelings catch up with me. My whole body burns. I shouldn't want to go hide, but I do.

I walk past my chair, past the class, through the lobby, and don't stop until I go into the bathroom and lock the stall door, my pulse throbbing in my neck like it's trying to escape my body.

I breathe in and out. I try to name my emotions, like Mr. Matt taught me. He calls it the Gut Check. What I'm feeling, and why.

First, I feel stupid for hiding in the bathroom. Again. I pat my sweaty face with toilet paper, waiting for my insides to stop moving like a stormy ocean. Whenever Zelia reads my stories, I have to hide my face until she's done, even though she always squeals with delight. This is like that, times a thousand. I'm embarrassed. Frightened. And also . . .

Delighted. *Delighted?* I ask myself. If I'm delighted, why did I book out of there like a zombie was after me?

A blissful kind of feeling fizzes in me, the same way I felt when Zelia and I played action figures when we were little. There's no time to do anything else, no time to think or tell myself I'm doing things wrong. Just time to be swept along this river of energy with the others. Not worrying about a thing.

I don't make any sense at all.

Someone enters and taps on the stall door. "Ava, sweetie, are you okay?" Miss Gwen says.

"Yeah." I flush the toilet with my foot, though I haven't done anything. "I just had to . . ."

"That was wonderful!" Miss Gwen's enthusiasm carries through the metal. "The details were superb. I loved how you presented the character's relationship to his parents and brother, and the problem he was having with his family." She pauses. "Actually, that's the hardest thing to teach. To have that realism."

I open the stall door. "So you got that it was a boy character?"

Miss Gwen's standing right outside. She grins. "Totally."

I wash my hands, blushing all over again. Pride. Another new emotion. Mr. Matt would be happy that I can name it.

Miss Gwen seems to understand that I need her to

stop going on about me because she does. She takes a few paper towels. "You know, I started doing improv when I was your age. I was having a really hard time at school. I never talked to anyone."

I rinse the soap off my hands. This doesn't seem possible. A teacher who was shy? Not to mention, Miss Gwen is a real live professional. Zelia says that everyone tells Miss Gwen she should move to LA or Chicago, where she can perform with some of the best companies in the world. "That's . . . weird."

Miss Gwen laughs. "It is kind of weird." She gives me the paper towels. "The thing I found about the stage is it's different from real life. I feel—I don't know. Safe up there." She shrugs. "Actually, a lot of us are introverts, if you can believe it."

I can't. Not really. Then again, I just managed to do something I never thought I could—say what was going through my head, like I was writing with my mouth instead of my fingers.

Who knows if I can ever do that again?

She puts a friendly arm around me. "Why don't you come back to class? You can sit and watch, if that's what you need."

I think about getting up there again, and I don't know. I did a good job once. I probably can't do it again. It's like the time I went on Space Mountain at Disneyland—I was glad I did it afterward, but I definitely did not want another turn. "I'll watch."

"Okay." Miss Gwen drops her arm and opens the bathroom door. I follow her inside. I consider dropping into a seat in the very back. My normal safe spot.

I decide to sit a little closer to the front. Just in case I change my mind.

I don't participate in the rest of the class, but nobody seems to care. Miss Gwen invites me back up but I shake my head and she doesn't push it. I watch them perform, my stomach swirling. Somehow watching it is worse than being in it.

After, I come out to find Dad chatting with the other parents. "I really ought to send Ryan to Cotillion," a tall woman with reddish hair like Ryan's, only long, is telling him.

"It's not too late. We'd love to have him," Dad answers. Then he sees me and puts his arm around me in a side hug. "How'd it go?"

I shrug. "It was okay."

"That probably means it was fantastic," Dad notes, and he and Ryan's mom laugh. He introduces me. "Ava, this is Mrs. Brighton."

I shake hands with her, trying to be firm but probably not being all that great, and turn back to Dad.

"Hey, Ryan." Cecily gives him a high five. "Good job today."

"Thank you very much." He turns to me and holds his hand. I hesitate, then slap it. "Hey, new girl. You were fantastic!" His voice echoes through the courtyard. "You must have done improv before."

I shake my head. His eyes, the color of Mom's lattes, widen. "Theater?" I shake it again.

Ryan goes very still. "Are you a movie star?"

Chad gasps and clutches his hand to his chest. "You know most movie stars can't improv." He starts running in circles around Ryan.

"Oh yeah? What about Amy Poehler? Steve Carell? Tina Fey?" Ryan names a bunch of other famous people.

Jonathan adjusts his glasses. "Indeed, many successful actors were improvisers first."

Ryan claps his hands like a teacher does for attention. "Folks, we have a ringer here. Cecily brought in a professional. How did you think of all that stuff to say for the character?"

My face gets so hot that I'm afraid I'll actually melt. Ryan is so . . . big. Not physically. I mean his personality. He seems like his volume is constantly turned up all the way, like a stereo that booms bass so loud you feel it in your stomach. I'm more like the mute button.

Ryan looks at me, waiting for a response. Chad is now doing some kind of robot dance behind him, his elbows bent. I shake my head instead of talking. My voice is all stopped up in the usual way, somewhere below my collarbone.

"It's her first time," Cecily says for me, to my relief.

"But she's a really good writer, and she always came with Zelia." She beams. "And her name's Ava, not New Girl."

It's interesting that Cecily said I'm a good writer, like Zelia did. Does that have anything to do with improv? I mean, I write with my fingers. But if I think about how I felt onstage and how I feel while I'm writing—they're kind of similar.

Except, of course, writing doesn't fill me with horrible fear or make me feel like I'm about to vomit when I'm just thinking about doing it. And I can rewrite all I like and I don't even have to share it with anyone if I don't want to.

Ryan grabs his chest and twirls around, gasping for air. Then he falls straight to the ground. "I am dead," he says. "You have killed me." He points at me. "It's not fair that you should be that good so fast."

Now I really need him to stop. My head burns like a coal and I turn around, hunching my shoulders. Luckily, Dad asks, "Ready, Ava?"

"Ready." I scurry over next to him, giving the kids an awkward wave I'm not sure they even notice.

"Let me know if you hear of a space that the theater can rent," Ryan's mom says to Dad. "I'll pass it along right away."

"Will do." Dad nods at Ryan's mom.

Dad and I walk away. "Rent a space for what?" I ask.

"Improv. Navegando Point raised their rent, so they have to move." Dad shakes his head. "The Port of San Diego wants to remodel this whole place."

I remember what happened with Dad's old warehouse. "Are they going to tear it all down like they did with your building?"

Dad nods. "Yes. In that case, the city council—or just one member of the city council, actually—called our businesses *blighted*. They said the buildings were eye-sores."

"And blighted means it's all old and run-down?" I guess.

"Right." Dad sighs. "But you know, I don't think everything has to be brand-new to be worthwhile. It makes it unaffordable for small businesses, especially industrial ones. Of all those businesses that used to be by Cotillion, I'm the only one still open. Nobody else could find a place they could afford."

A pang hits my chest as I remember the woodworker and the other shops that used to be by Cotillion. I was little when all that happened, so I didn't really care that much.

What if the theater goes under, too? Or what if they have to move somewhere far away, and Dad can't take me? "Do you know of any spaces the theater can rent?"

"No. Theater spaces are hard to find. I'm always booked a year in advance, so it's pretty easy for me to

plan ahead. Plus, they need rehearsal and class space."
Dad looks at his watch. "Anyway, that's not for you to
worry about. Want some ice cream?"

"Um, is that even a question?" Forgetting about the
theater for now, I run ahead of him toward the sound
of the carousel music playing "In the Good Old Summertime." It sounds like a giant windup music box. The
ice-cream shop is right next to it. It's more of a stand,
really—you walk up to the window and order, then sit at
one of the tables outdoors.

I round the corner into the big courtyard and skid to
a halt. The shutters are pulled tight across the opening
of the ice-cream stand. Closed.

"Why's it closed?" I don't understand. It's a Saturday.
"Did they run out?"

Dad walks around the stand, as if it will tell him a
different answer. "I guess their rent got raised, too." He
shakes his head and gestures around. "I walked around
and counted ten stores that are out of business, including the Greek place with the good gyros."

I look at the little kids on the carousel and feel sorry
for them because they won't get ice cream afterward,
like I used to. "What about the cupcake shop?" It's in
another area over by the duck pond.

Dad and I go investigate, passing store after dark
store with their doors tightly shut. My pulse speeds.
Please be open, I pray for the cupcakes. "But what are

they going to do when all the stores close? There will be nothing here at all."

All these people with no jobs, no new place to open. What are they all going to do?

Dad frowns. "I think they're putting in a hotel or something."

"Ew." I think about the hotels I've seen. If you're not staying there you can't exactly hang out by them.

We walk by the duck pond, which has a wooden bridge going over it. There are just two ducks in there, quacking sadly. The water's kind of green, even for a pond. It's like they're just letting everything go.

I head to the building where the cupcake shop is, turning into the corridor lined with shops. I breathe a sigh of relief when I smell the sugary chocolate wafting out of the area and see their lights on, covering the hallway in a warm glow. "Thank goodness."

A woman stands behind the counter in a white blouse and hairnet, frosting cupcakes with gloved hands. "May I help you?" She smiles. She's younger than Mom by maybe ten years and has red hair.

I practically press my nose against the glass case. Chocolate. Vanilla. Even pineapple. How can I choose? I give Dad a pleading look. "I think we should get some for Luke and Hudson, too."

Dad arches a brow. "Why not?"

"Oh boy." I almost do a little jump, except that I'm in front of a stranger.

The woman's smile gets bigger, which makes mine get bigger, too. "I've got a son about your age," she says. "Are you twelve?"

"In February." I stand taller. It always makes me happy when people think I'm older than I am. Dad says that'll change later.

"Tell her what kinds you want, Ava," Dad says, and I start pointing. I keep waiting for him to say enough, but he doesn't—he must feel bad about the shops closing, too. And that's how we walk out of Navegando Point with a half-dozen cupcakes.

CHAPTER 9

"Check this out!" Zelia chirps. It's Sunday morning and we're FaceTiming. She holds up her dark hair. It's got bright pink and blue streaks.

"Wow! That looks like cotton candy." I admire the colors. "Amazing."

"Thanks." She holds up a handful. "Lottie had to bleach it and then dye it. Took forever."

A small surge of jealousy punches me in the gut. "Who's Lottie? Your hairdresser?"

"My friend Tristan's older sister." Zelia holds the hair over her lip like a mustache. "You'd like Tristan. He's in my theater club. He's the youngest, but he's such a good actor."

Is Tristan taking my place? But I want her to be happy. Zelia's making new friends. "That's cool." I have something to tell her, too. I swallow. "Oh, by the way, I'm doing improv now."

I wait for her to be amazed.

"I know. Your mom told my mom." Zelia pushes her hair over her face.

My happiness pops like a balloon. I want her to acknowledge me. To say, *Hey, I know that must have been really hard for you. I'm proud.* Or at least say something.

It's hard to tell on FaceTime, but I think maybe she's a little sad. Her eyes seem to turn down at the corners like sideways commas. "Do the improv kids miss me?"

"Yeah!" I say, though truthfully nobody mentioned her except the one time at the beginning. I don't think Jonathan or Babel were in the class with her at all. It makes me feel a little guilty. "Are you going to start an improv group in your new town?"

Zelia sniffles as if she's getting over a cold. "No. I think I've moved past it."

My stomach feels like an ice cube. "What do you mean, you've moved past it?"

"Theater people don't really think of improv as real acting."

She's using her know-it-all voice. I remember another time when Zelia acted like this. We were in fourth grade and I brought Barbies over to her house to play. She looked at them, sniffed, and said, "I'm kind of over dolls, Ava. They're a little immature, don't you think?" But then I found out she said that because her older cousin told her that.

I make a guess. "So your new theater club doesn't like improv?"

She shakes her head. "Nope. They said it doesn't count."

"They kind of sound like jerks," I say, surprising myself at how definite I sound. "You loved improv."

She moves her hair out of her face and rubs her eyes. "Now that I've done real acting, I can see what they mean."

Improv isn't real acting? I think it's real. It's just different. And it seems like it would help regular acting, wouldn't it? Ryan and Jonathan pointed out all the famous actors who started in improv. I can't help feeling insulted, but I don't know what to say without sounding mad. I touch the scar on my chest, my fingertips running over the smooth-rough surface under my collarbone, feeling the wires that come out of the artery bumping up against my skin.

I wait for Zelia to notice the look on my face and me doing my little anxious thing. But she looks right at me and I see something flicker over her face. Like someone who's just understood a math problem, she knows what I'm feeling.

Yet she says nothing about it. Instead, Zelia pulls her hair back and changes the subject. "Is it warm there?" She puts her hoodie over her head. "It's starting to be really cold. My nose is running so much I can't stand it." She takes a tissue out of a box, blows. It sounds like a car horn.

I glance out the window at the sun beating down on the tree, remembering that Dad asked me to water it today. "It's nice and warm today. I'm wearing shorts."

We sink into silence, both of us looking at something random off our screens.

"You know, you don't have to do improv just because I did," Zelia says at last.

I frown. Does she not want me to do it? "I know that. But you always said it helped you in other ways. Remember? Like in talking with people."

She shrugs. "That's probably more me than improv. You know I'm an extrovert."

My heart speeds up. So she doesn't think it'll help me? I'm not sure what's going on with this conversation, but I know one thing. Time to change the subject. I blow out a breath. "So what does a Maine accent sound like?"

Zelia leans forward. "They're like, *It's not summah time anymoah.*" She launches into a monologue about the weather as I listen. We spend the rest of the time talking about that, and how people either think Zelia must be totally cool or entirely awful because she's from California. Nothing we talk about is bad. But nothing is super great, either. It's like talking to a stranger at Cotillion. Polite. Calm. Boring.

She's too far away. Things are changing between us, and I have to think of a way to stop it.

CHAPTER 10

The next morning, I'm standing on the basketball court, wishing I could still be in bed instead of out here, waiting for directions. It's only second period and I already forgot my lunch and dropped my science assignment in the hallway—I had to turn it in covered in footprints. I could use a Monday do-over.

Of all the classes I wish I didn't have to take, PE tops the list. Theoretically it should be easy-peasy. Just change into baggy maroon pants and a gray T-shirt and stand around with the other sixth-grade PE class, waiting for stuff to happen. After changing in the locker room, doing the roll call, and getting things explained to us, we usually end up with maybe twenty minutes of actual sport time, if we're lucky.

But sometimes we actually have to do work. Like today.

The morning sky is still overcast and cool. The smell

of the grassy lower field combined with the dirt smell of the baseball diamond makes me a little nauseous, like it always does, because it means something I don't want to do is about to happen. In the dirt surrounding the blacktop, squirrels run around, not even caring that a bunch of middle schoolers are right in front of them. If any of us move, they just jump into one of the many burrows.

I wish I could follow them.

Ty's in this class, too. So far I've been able to avoid talking to him or looking at him, but I don't know if that will last forever.

The two teachers set up orange lines of cones on opposite ends of the basketball court. There are two sixth-grade PE classes, so the teachers usually like to team up in one lesson. My teacher is Mrs. Balding, who says she's been here for a hundred years, though she went to school with Dad. She moves slowly, like an injured sloth, sighing as though putting out the orange cones is the hardest thing she ever did.

Ms. Evans, the other sixth-grade teacher, puts down her cones, then scurries toward us like a squirrel who's had too much coffee, stopping right as she gets to the front row. Some of the kids shriek-laugh. "You ready for this?" Ms. Evans shouts and claps, like we're in some kind of nightclub instead of standing on a field. This is her first teaching job and she's a little too enthusiastic, if you ask me.

"Yeah," we mutter.

She puts a hand over her ear. "That was weak! Let me hear some energy!"

"YEAH!" the other kids shout. I pretend to shout, but I don't make a sound.

Mrs. Balding turns over a big orange bucket and lowers herself onto it. "Let's just get on with it." She takes a sip of coffee out of a giant 7-Eleven mug.

"You know what today is?" Ms. Evans points at the cones. "PACER test. PACER stands for Progressive Aerobic Cardiovascular Endurance Run."

Cardiovascular? I swallow. That can't be okay for me, can it? Then again, my doctor didn't excuse me from anything. He says as long as I don't do a marathon I'll be okay. I do the mile and stuff. I just do it slowly.

Mrs. Balding says, "This is just a test to see how your personal cardio is. It is not a race. There is no winner."

The kids murmur. A kind of discomfort ripples through my abdomen. It's not a race but it feels like a competition. And I'm not good at competition.

Ms. Evans counts off ten of us. Including me. "Stand on this line."

Great. I should have hidden in the back. I go put my toes on the white painted stripe on the asphalt.

"What you're going to do is just run to the other cones, where we've drawn the line." She takes a small wireless speaker out of her pocket. "When you hear a beep, the lap is over. When you hear the triple beat, that's the signal that it's going to get faster." She holds up a hand. "Now, if you don't get back to the line before the beep, it won't count. If it happens twice, you're out. Okay?" Ms. Evans touches a button on her phone.

"The PACER test will begin in thirty seconds," a voice says through the speaker.

The other kids get in a ready stance. I imitate them, though I feel as if my feet have grown roots through the asphalt. I put my palm over my chest. I mean, the doctor would excuse me from PE if I couldn't do this, right? He said not to get my pulse up too high. The pacemaker won't do anything unless my pulse gets really, really fast and then stays that high, or goes into an irregular rhythm.

What if my heart stops right here in front of everyone?

I almost raise my hand to get Mrs. Balding's attention, when I hear a voice I recognize muttering. "She'll get out of it. Watch."

Ty.

If this were the old days when Alexander Hamilton was alive, this would be like challenging me to a duel. Like slapping gloves across my face or whatever they did. I grit my teeth. Now if I don't do it, I'll be proving Ty's point.

I push my worries aside and clench my teeth. I'll show him.

The voice intones, "Start."

The other kids start jogging slowly to the other line. Okay, this isn't so bad. I get there only a little bit behind the others. We wait.

BEEP.

We run back to the other side. The world jiggles as my feet pound the earth, making me feel dizzy. Crud. I slow down. The kids on the sideline stare at me. Ty smirks. My chest burns. But I'm not sure if that's because of my heart or the smirk. They're thinking, *Really? On the first lap?*

BEEP.

The sound goes off before I reach the line.

"That's one missed," Mrs. Balding says from her upside-down bucket.

I get to the line, my skin hot, as if the stares are coals burning me.

BEEP BEEP BEEP.

"It's a little faster now," Ms. Evans calls. "You can do it, Ava!"

My heart's beating so fast. Dr. White always tells me not to worry about my heart because the device will do its job. "It's there so you can do *more* things, not fewer," he always says. "You just live your life." But I can't help worrying. My fingers go up to my neck, for my pulse. Steady. Fast, but steady. That's good.

My feet slow even more. I concentrate on the asphalt, how my scuffed white shoes look against the darkness of it. I hear the kids snickering. They don't know about my heart. Why would they? I look perfectly normal from the outside. You can't see my scar most of the time.

Still, it's not okay for them to laugh. If I were braver, I'd tell them so. If Zelia were here, I wouldn't even be doing this. She would have roared at the teachers for even making me try.

BEEΓ.

I'm not even close to the line.

"You're out, Ava," Mrs. Balding says. She knows about my heart, but she hasn't let me get out of stuff. I don't know if it's because she thinks I can secretly do everything or if she's trying to be encouraging.

I slink away, my head down.

"Don't worry about it," Ms. Evans calls after me. "It's only a personal time. It doesn't count against you." She doesn't know about my heart because she's not my teacher. I feel like I've disappointed her. I want to explain why I couldn't do it, but I'd rather poke myself with a cactus spike. She'll look at me sympathetically and tell me it's okay, and everyone will watch, and I'll feel a million times worse.

Mrs. Balding gestures Ms. Evans over. I watch them whisper. They glance over at me. This makes all the other kids glance over at me, too.

If the world were going to end, now would be a great time.

I pass Ty, who's standing with his arms crossed and

his eyes narrowed into a glare. *Faker*, I hear him think, and I turn my sweaty face away. I'm not a faker.

Am I?

Dr. White says it's okay to do PE, and he says not to worry. Maybe I could have tried harder. Pushed a little more. I probably gave up too soon.

Ms. Evans comes back, a slight frown furrowing her brow. "Great job, Ava." She gives me a fist bump. "Tell you what. Hang out by the locker room and catch your breath. Then you can walk some slow laps around the basketball court if you want. Okay?"

I glance at Ty and catch his eye again. He glares and I look away. It's not like I'm happy about any of this. It just feels like I'm not good enough. Again.

"Okay." I go over to the building and slump down on the concrete, the pink stucco wall sticking into my back, and watch the other kids for the rest of the hour.

CHAPTER 11

"**H**ow many turtles?" Mr. Matt crinkles his already crinkly eyes at me from his oversized yellow chair. It's an hour after school, and I'm at my monthly therapy appointment.

I'm looking out the second-story window, down behind the building. There's water running there at the bottom of a hill. He calls it a river, but it's really a concrete run-off ditch. So it'd be a stream or a creek, not a river, if you want to get technical about it.

Though it's totally man-made, there are plants and turtles and fish as if it's a real stream and not just water from the occasional rain or the sprinklers from the people up the ridge. I guess nature tries to find a way to survive no matter what.

"I count three turtles." This is our routine. I tell him how many of each creature I see. I know why he does it—(a) so I'll relax and (b) because when I'm anxious he wants me to notice things around me.

"Really? I only saw one yesterday." Mr. Matt cranes his head over his desk to look.

"There are three today." I sit on the blue couch and pick up the red stress ball and begin squishing it.

"How's school?" he asks. I look up at him, taking in his dreads neatly pulled back with a colorful blue-and-white scarf, his pressed khakis, his spiffy brown shoes.

I shrug. What am I supposed to do, give him a complete rundown of everything that happened today? Ty flashes into my head and I give him the boot. I don't need to think about him, though every time I have to talk to him I feel like I'm about to be questioned by a judge or something. Instead, I tell him about PE.

"You tried it." He nods with a smile. "That's something to be proud of."

I shake my head, unable to get out all my thoughts through my mouth. I don't tell him about how what I feel and what the doctor said don't match. Or about Ty or the other kids.

"It was always Zelia who encouraged you at school. How are you doing with her absence?" Mr. Matt asks.

I shrug again. "It's still weird. I mean, I talk to her on FaceTime or Skype. But it's not the same." I don't explain how it feels like I'm nothing without her. Like she was the engine in my car. And how, with her new pink-and-blue hair and her theater, she feels like a totally different person with a different life.

"Friendships can change with distance."

I swallow. Ours wasn't supposed to. We were supposed to go to college together. Live next door to each other. Go to the retirement home together. "I guess."

"It's important to allow your friendships room to evolve. Be open and supportive."

I squish the squishy ball and tune him out. I don't come here to be lectured. I can get that at home.

"How do you feel about the change, Ava?" He crosses his legs, waiting for me.

I don't want to talk about Zelia anymore. Last time I was here, right after school started, I spent the whole session crying about her and felt awful afterward. I change the subject.

"I might have made a new friend." I tell him about Cecily, and how she asked me to do improv.

Mr. Matt's eyes widen and he almost jumps out of his chair. "Shut the front door!" he nearly shouts, and I roll my eyes at his corniness. "Improv? That's great!"

I look at my fingernails, thinking of improv and how it made me want to run away and do more of it at the same time. "I don't know if I'll go back."

"It'll be good for you, Ava," Mr. Matt says. "Do you know that there are improv classes for anxiety? I've only seen them for adults or I would've sent you."

I sigh impatiently. I don't care if a billion people do improv for anxiety.

"What's the worst that can happen?" Mr. Matt counters. That's his favorite question.

"I go there again, and Cecily ignores me, and they all ignore me because they secretly hated me and were only being polite the first time." I move my shoulders up and down.

"Then you don't have to return." He leans back and looks at me. "You're good at making up stories."

I nod, wondering what his point is. "So I've heard."

"But you tend to make up negative ones—you think of all the bad things that could happen. However . . ." He widens his eyes again. He's got very expressive eyes. "It's just as possible that the stories could be positive. Things could end well. So why not make up positive stories about what might happen?"

This hits me like a small punch to my gut. I grunt. "I guess I'm wrong, then."

"You're not wrong, Ava. Just tell me—what's the *best* thing that could happen?"

I know what he wants me to say. That I'll have a great time. Everything will be sunny and full of rainbow goodness. I try to make my mouth form the words, but suddenly it seems there's a brick wall between my brain and my tongue.

I get up and go look at the turtles instead of answering.

CHAPTER 12

I try as hard as I can to be invisible. It's our second improv class, and the other kids are sitting up front in the theater. I sit in the sixth row. Nobody notices I came in—they all have their backs turned, so they would have to completely swivel around to see me.

I bite down on a hangnail, rip it off. Exactly the thing Zelia told me not to do. Zelia's into manicures—her specialty is leopard spots. "How you treat your nails gives *me* anxiety," she'd say. But no matter how many leopard spots Zelia painted on my nails, I just couldn't keep from chipping or peeling them within a day.

Now my nails haven't been painted since she left. I sigh a little. If Zelia were here, I wouldn't be sitting alone. She'd be telling me how these kids really feel about me because I can't seem to figure it out.

Just then, a man and a woman in what Dad calls "business casual" dress (tan pants and button-up shirts) walk into the theater. The man has a buzz cut and looks like he'd always play an FBI agent in the movies. The woman has what my brothers call the *can I talk to the manager?* face, like she's permanently unhappy with life and wants to complain about it to someone. She glances around the theater as if we're inside a dumpster in a back alley. Her makeup is perfectly done and kind of heavy, like the ladies who work at the cosmetic counters inside department stores.

I dislike both of them right away, though I don't know why.

Miss Gwen stops them at the doorway. "Can I help you?" she asks in a low voice.

"We're from the Brancusi Group, out of New York," the woman says, smiling. "I'm Brett Rosselin."

I sit up straight. The developers are here. I turn my head so I'm not looking at them directly, like a spy.

"We're here to invite you to one of our community forums." The man hands Miss Gwen a flyer. He doesn't introduce himself. "There are two different dates. The first one is an informal meeting here in Navegando Point, and the second is a public hearing at the Port of San Diego in November."

Miss Gwen folds it in half without glancing at it. "We already got an eviction notice. What difference does it make?"

Brett, like some kind of robot mannequin, doesn't blink. "I'm sure we can help you find a spot within our new development."

"In between Gucci and Prada stores?" Miss Gwen sets the paper on the chair, and looks back at them with a tight smile.

"Listen." Brett gets closer to Miss Gwen. "You can tell the owner of the theater that we can work together or apart. We *want* to work together."

I stare at the floor. Weird that she's saying she wants to work together, but somehow it sounds like a threat.

Miss Gwen wrinkles her nose. "Well, you can tell your manager that when he stops giving kickbacks to our elected officials, we can talk about what's fair and what's not."

"We don't do that," the woman says quickly. "We are completely aboveboard."

The man takes Brett by the elbow. "Thank you for your time, ma'am." Brett turns back, her mouth opening and closing as if she wants to say something.

Miss Gwen calls, "Please shut the door after you! Thank you."

I bet they're not really going to find her a spot "within our new development." Not in between all those fancy stores. I want to ask Miss Gwen if it's true, but my throat clams up. My teacher shakes her whole body from her shoulders down and writes a note on her clipboard. "Ugh," she mutters. Then she notices me. "Ava! What are you doing way in the back?"

"Ummm . . ." My whole body heats up. Now the kids turn and look. Something like hurt flashes over Cecily's face, and suddenly I understand that Cecily doesn't dislike me at all. My stomach free-falls into the center of the earth. Great. Now Cecily thinks I'm a snob, not wanting to sit with them.

I get up and move to the second row, right behind Cecily. My heart pounds in my stomach. She sits facing forward, listening to Miss Gwen talk about what we're going to do that day. I have to do something. Make the first move, or she'll think I hate her. I tap on her shoulder. "Hi," I whisper.

She flashes her grin over her shoulder. "Hey. Glad you came back." She reaches a hand out, and I high-five it, and I forget about the Brancusi people for now.

"Kids, I want you to know that the theater has to move out of this space next week," Miss Gwen tells us. "We'll be renting a classroom space at a public library to finish the class."

"Already?" Ryan says. "My mom's been looking . . ."

"They doubled our rent a few months ago." Miss Gwen blinks rapidly. "We're in the process of finding a new space. But I don't want you to worry! Our community is too strong to just go away, okay?" She stares at us as if she expects a response.

"Okay," we all chorus.

"Now get up on stage and let's do some improv!" Miss Gwen claps.

* * *

I want to worry about the theater situation, but it turns out when you do improv, all you can do is concentrate on what you're actually doing. Miss Gwen makes us stand in a circle. She's holding a small blow-up beach ball striped in red and yellow. "It's Loser Ball time!" she says, and the other kids clap. I don't. This isn't going to be good. I'm terrible at anything that requires hand-eye coordination.

"This is how it works. I throw it to someone." She tosses it to Cecily, who, instead of catching it, turns around and lets it hit her on the bottom. "You don't catch it. But we all cheer."

Everyone's applauding and hooting. "Yay, Cecily! Woo-hoo!" Ryan shouts. "You'll get it next time."

Cecily throws it at Chad, who hits it with his head. Again we cheer. I worry about what I'll do. Maybe I'll do it wrong anyway.

Then Chad throws it to me.

Without thinking, I crumple to the ground as the ball hits my chest. "Yay, Ava!" the class shouts. "Way to go! You'll get it next time."

Cecily gives me a hand up. I throw the ball to Ryan, who lets it bounce off his chest. We shout again, and my voice is loud in a way it hasn't been since Zelia moved. "Go Ryan!" I yell. "Woo-hoo!"

I don't have to be good at this game. I'm not *supposed* to be good at this game. It's okay to mess up.

"I want you to approach improv like this game." Miss Gwen does a weird shimmy that knocks the ball across the room. Chad runs to get it. "The more you mess up, the more fun it is. And everyone will support you no matter what. Nothing bad will happen." She smiles at me and I smile back.

For the first time in my whole life, I'm almost not afraid to do something wrong in front of other people. The knotted-up thing in my stomach relaxes. Loser Ball is the best ball game of all time.

CHAPTER 13

On Monday, Mr. Sukow assigns us a long-term project. Ads. We're supposed to write a commercial for a product, and then perform it for the class. Oral presentations, my worst nightmare. I want another option. Why can't I just write a script? Or a story about the product?

"They should be thirty seconds long, and they should convey what they are and why you should buy them." Mr. Sukow hands us the rubric, a sheet telling us what we need to do to get an A. Besides those things he just named, it also needs to be typed up in a specific script-writing Google app on our Chromebooks so we can share it with him. It's due in five weeks. "You'll work on it occasionally in class, but otherwise work on it at home. You may use video if you choose, but this will take extra time." He pauses dramatically. "Do not, I repeat, *do not* leave it all until the last minute."

"Why are you encouraging us to be capitalists?" Ty pipes up from behind me. "What if we don't want to encourage people to buy products they don't need?"

"Because you actually do need these. Everyone does." Mr. Sukow puts a large cardboard box on his desk and begins pulling out the products. "Besides, would you rather do two dozen grammar worksheets or this fun project?" He grins. Ty's kind of a smart aleck, and it bugs some teachers, but Mr. Sukow seems to like him. I personally think Ty could turn it down like ten notches.

Mr. Sukow dramatically pulls each item out and sets them on the desk. There's a sponge, a coffee cup, a long-handled umbrella, and a brown paper napkin.

"Ugh. Those are boring," Ty pipes up.

"That's the point." Mr. Sukow folds the plain brown napkin in half. "That's the challenge. To make these boring objects appealing. Got it?"

I stare at the rubric. It does say, *Make object sound interesting.* How do you do that with a paper napkin?

"And you'll be working with partners," Mr. Sukow says in a cheerful tone, as if this is the best idea anyone's ever had in the history of ideas.

The classroom starts buzzing. That changes everything. Cecily turns to me and points, then points at herself. I nod, smiling, my hopes soaring. This will be fun. Like working with Zelia. Cecily can do the presentation and I'll just write it.

"Assigned partners," Mr. Sukow amends, and everyone groans. "And you will tell me what grade you think the other deserves, so make sure you all pull your weight." He starts pointing at people, telling them who's with who.

"Napkins," he says. "Ava." I hold my breath, hoping he points to Cecily next, but he says, "Ty. You're partners."

"Noooooo," Ty groans, and for once I pretty much agree with him. He's no prize, either. But I would never say that out loud like he did. Obviously Ty's never been to Cotillion.

My mind flashes back to improv. Miss Gwen told us that when we get a suggestion, we always have to say *thank you*. "Be grateful for it, or the whole audience will feel bad," she had said. "Even if you think it's the most horrible suggestion in the history of all time." Then she made us each practice saying thank you.

Ty being assigned to me is like getting one of those bad suggestions.

"Thank you!" I say, ridiculously loud, before I think about it too much, and the class snickers like I'm being sarcastic. But I'm not. Ty swivels in his seat to look at me. I try to smile at him.

A sneer wrinkles his pale face. Then he tosses his head onto his desk with a thunk. "Kill me now."

I sink way down into my seat. I wonder if it's too

late in the year to switch out of English class or change schools. Or move out of the country.

After the last bell, I'm walking out of the building when Cecily catches up. "So I take it you and Ty aren't exactly friends."

"That's an understatement." I'd spent the rest of the period looking up napkins. Which did not tell me anything new. Except that there haven't been any new napkin inventions in forever. I mean, what else could they do to a napkin?

All I want to do is go to my grandparents' house and have a giant bowl of ice cream so I can put this day behind me. I have to turn right, walk through the park, and I'll be there in no time. I begin to veer, expecting Cecily to keep going straight. "Bye, Cecily."

She doesn't change direction. "I'll walk with you through the park. I'm not getting a ride today."

Oh. A little shiver of happiness zips through me. I smile at her and she smiles back. Am I making a friend? My stomach jumps. What should I say?

We continue on in silence through the school parking lot. Cecily doesn't seem to mind my quiet. I relax a little.

Ryan's in the park, jumping around on the grass like a golden retriever that's been turned into a boy, his hair flopping back and forth. If he had a long, feathery tail he'd be wagging it. "Aaahhh! Free at last."

Chad runs circles around him. "I thought this day would never end!"

Around them are some other boys I don't know. They're all talking and laughing. Looking at these strangers, I close up like a clamshell inside.

"Hi, Ryan! Hi, Chad!" Cecily calls out. They wave and smile.

I try to smile at them, but I can't make myself meet their eyes. Instead I find myself getting sweaty. Eye contact is a thing Mr. Matt is trying to work with me on. He says it makes me have a fear response and the only way to get over it is to . . . (drumroll) make eye contact.

Obviously not going to happen.

Anyway, I'm not sure whether Ryan and Chad actually like me or if they were just being nice during improv. They sure don't want to talk to me right now—they're with their real friends. Who definitely don't want to hang out with me. They haven't even smiled or looked over.

"You!" Ryan races over. "New girl!"

"Ava," Cecily corrects him, like she did during improv.

Chad pants, his hands on his thighs. "Dude, stop moving so fast." There's a noise like a full, churning garbage disposal, and Chad claps his hand over his belly.

"Was that you?" Cecily asks.

"I thought someone was flushing a toilet!" Ryan giggles.

I turn red on Chad's behalf. If my stomach did that in front of people, I would have to go hide forever.

"It totally sounded like that." Chad doesn't look the least bit embarrassed. "Oh, man. I'm so hungry."

Ryan regards the rest of us. "Anybody want to go to Fosters Freeze?"

Fosters Freeze is a couple blocks away. They sell soft-serve ice cream and burgers and things like that. For all of elementary school, Zelia and I wanted to walk to Fosters Freeze on our own, but our parents said we had to wait until we were in middle school.

Then, of course, Zelia moved away, so I thought my dreams of getting a dipped cone after school were dead. I'm probably supposed to ask my parents' permission or something first, but won't they just be happy that I'm doing things with real people? Nobody else is trying to ask their parents.

"Yeah!" one of the other boys bellows, and like a wave they all start moving toward the store, Ryan and Chad and Cecily with them. Only I stand still, undecided. What if they really didn't want me to go after all?

"I gotta get home," I say to the air, and walk in the opposite direction.

"No Fosters Freeze?" Ryan calls after me. He sounds disappointed, maybe.

"Come on, Ava!" Cecily adds. "It'll be fun."

For a moment I slow down. It's hot today. A soft-serve vanilla-chocolate cone dipped in chocolate would taste so good right now, and I have a folded five-dollar bill in the inner pocket of my backpack. *You always wanted to go after school*, my mind reminds me. *What's the big deal?*

No, my gut tells me it's safer if I don't go. "Sorry. My grandparents will get worried."

I break into a run, my huge backpack smacking my spine like a cartoon anvil.

I run for exactly thirty seconds before I'm winded and slow down to a walk. No wonder I'm terrible at the PACER.

I text Zelia, almost automatically.

Hey, I just did something kind of stupid, I think. I ran away from Fosters Freeze and the improv kids and I'm pretty sure they hate me now. What should I do?

I wait. Probably she'll tell me to just go back. But she doesn't respond—it's dinnertime there. I sigh and pocket my phone.

"Hey," someone calls from the grass. It's Luke. "Going to Jichan's?" He crosses over to me.

"Yeah," I say. I can still see the group, walking in a diagonal direction across the park.

"Text me if they have butter pecan," he says, then follows my eyes. "Did they ditch you?"

I shake my head. "I, uh, they're going to Fosters Freeze."

Luke sighs. "Ava. You didn't freak out again, did you? You have to be tough!"

My heart leaps and I clench my hands into fists. "It's a little bit more complicated than being tough." Luke never even tries to understand.

"It's not. Point your body that way and go catch up. That's it." Luke puts his hands on my shoulders and turns me so I'm facing the group.

I turn away. I could explain how I feel for fifty days and nights and he'll never understand me. "See you. And I'm *not* texting you. If you want butter pecan, you'll have to come see for yourself whether they have it."

"Fine," he calls after me, and I stomp off.

My grandparents' house is only a few blocks away from the school, less than a quarter mile. My grandfather's sitting cross-legged on the small green lawn with a big straw beach hat, the kind that lifeguards wear, on his head.

"Hi, Jīchan!" I wave.

He's holding a pair of manicure scissors in his hands and snipping away at his grass. Some people think this is weird, but my grandfather is very particular about his yard. So he'll sit there and yank up tiny weeds and trim the grass that his lawn mower missed with tiny manicure scissors. Mom says it's a harmless hobby. Jīchan ran his own landscaping company for years and years, so now the only yard he has to fuss over is his own.

I step through the picket fence—Jīchan put it up so neighbor dogs can't pee on his nice lawn—and he looks up. "Ava-chan!" He beams up at me from under his big hat. "I bought Moose Tracks! They had a good ice-cream sale."

"Oh boy!" I lean down and give him a peck on his tanned cheek. Nana Linda makes him wear the hat, so I know she's home.

"I'll be in as soon as I finish this row." He points to some slightly uneven grass that nobody except him would notice. He peers up, listening to my still-hard breathing. "Were you running?"

"Just a little."

Worry passes over his face like a cloud. I have the same condition my grandmother had. That's how she died. "Your grandmother always missed the days when she could run. Enjoy it."

While you can, I add in my head because I know that's what he's thinking. My grandmother was more or less okay when she was a kid, and then she got sick as a grown-up. Jīchan means well, but sometimes being around him makes me think too much about my heart, and the bad things that could happen to it in the future.

The doctor says it's not necessarily true that I'll be exactly like my grandmother. They caught my condition early; they didn't know about hers for a long time because noncompaction cardiomyopathy is kind of a newly discovered thing. They just thought she had a randomly weak heart. I'm much better off than her because they have better medicines and treatments now. I get an echocardiogram that looks at my heart every year and I take baby aspirin to prevent blood clots. I might also get this procedure called an abla-tion, which will zap away the irregular heartbeats, but that's in a "wait and see" phase right now.

That's what Mom and Dad tell me. And that's what I have to keep focused on or I'll want to hide under my covers for the rest of my days.

I pat my grandfather's hat. "Don't worry about me."

"Might as well tell me to stop breathing." He chuck-les, but catches my hand and squeezes it.

I step into the small living room and kick off my shoes. The room's kind of dark, with most of the light coming from a picture window by the dining area, which over-looks a valley dotted with houses. The walls are lined with photos of my mom, her mom, and Jīchan. New pho-tos of Nana Linda with all of us are there, too, plus Nana Linda's children and grandchildren. I bet strangers are confused by the variety of people in these.

Nana Linda's relaxing in her recliner, crocheting a hat and watching some kind of farming documentary. "Hi, munchkin." She hits the lever and pops herself upright, standing up and adjusting her crocheted vest and colorful leggings. "How are you?"

I let her pull me into a hug and she kisses the top of my head. Nana Linda's my step-grandma. She and Jīchan got married seven years ago. Nana Linda has six grandchildren courtesy of her own grown-up children, and thus has plenty of grandma experience, but none of them live in town.

Jīchan is seventy and five years younger than his wife, but Nana Linda actually seems like the younger one. She has silver hair that used to be bright red when she was young, styled into a sleek bob, and her makeup's always on point. A yoga and dance teacher, she moves like a much younger person. She smells like coconut, like she's just been to the beach.

I think about improv and how scary and fun that was, and then about how I have to work with Ty, and how I just ran away from those kids instead of going to Fosters Freeze.

But I don't tell her any of this. "I'm okay." Telling her all my thoughts after I've been doing nothing but play- ing them over and over in my head feels exhausting. Not to mention how Luke made me feel. I don't want to talk to anyone right now.

She arches a brow. "Just okay?"

I nod.

She puts her arm around me and we walk like a

three-legged race into the kitchen. "Let's have some ice cream and you can tell me about it."

Nana Linda only eats ice cream when I come over. She says it's a way to limit her ice-cream intake. Too bad for her because I'm here almost every day. They also have a TV plan with more channels than we have, so I record this one anime show we don't get and watch it here.

To change the subject, I ask her how she is, and she tells me a little bit about the Yoga for Seniors class she leads at the rec center. "I got a woman who uses a cane to be in warrior pose for a full minute!" she says proudly. That's a pose where you basically do a lunge with your legs, and have your arms out horizontally, and you have to hold it until your thighs collapse out from under you. At least, that's what I do.

"Wow. That's great." I sound fake because I'm still thinking about Fosters Freeze.

"So everything's just *okay*. But tell me about improv." Nana Linda opens the freezer drawer and gets out five different flavors of ice cream. They always have too much. "Which kind?"

"A little of each, please." I need to make her think about something else. "Improv's okay." She'll ask me about my feelings forever and try therapy on me. I get enough therapy with Mr. Matt. I wash my hands, soaping them up really well to my elbows. My arms always smell funky after school from leaning on the desks that other people have been using all day.

Finally, I hit on inspiration. Something that will make her get fired up and forget all about me and my feelings. "Do you hear what's happening with Navegando Point?" I tell her about the redevelopment and how all those stores are already closed. Social issues always do the trick.

Nana Linda's expression grows stormy and I know I was correct. "I thought it got canceled because it's a historic site."

"I don't know about that part, but it's definitely on. I mean, otherwise stores wouldn't have closed, right?" I dry my hands and arms. With any luck, she'll forget all about asking me personal questions.

"Right," she says, and looks thoughtful. I take the ice-cream bowl and go sit down in the dining area that's open to the kitchen. Nana Linda opens her laptop.

Jichan hangs up his hat by the front door as he comes in. "What'd I miss?"

Nana Linda whirls to him. "They're going to tear down Navegando Point and put in a huge, ugly, awful hotel and fancy shops and ruin the harbor!"

"Slow down." Jichan holds up his hands.

"Well. We need to do something about it."

My stomach roils as though I'm on a boat. Uh-oh. Maybe that wasn't the right thing to bring up.

Nana Linda can be a little hard to deal with some-times. She gets an idea and she starts forcing everyone to do it. Last year, she made my brothers and me go to the women's march, which was too noisy and crowded for me. She's like Zelia's grandma, who makes Zelia go to church and stuff, except with causes.

I thought Nana Linda would just *talk* about Nave-gando Point, not actually make me do something. I spoon ice cream into my mouth, focusing on the cold creaminess. I wonder what the others are eating at Fos-ters Freeze right now.

They're probably relieved I didn't go so they don't have to look at me sitting there all awkward and silent.

"Here." Nana Linda turns the screen around for me. "This Facebook page, Rescue Navegando Point Now!, is the only thing I can find about it. Plus some news arti-cles about how great it will be."

"Aren't newspapers not supposed to take sides?" Mr. Sukow had us do an assignment on bias, where we read the same news story from multiple places and compared them. You'd think the news would be all facts, but every-one has a different spin on what happens.

Nana Linda nods. "That's how it should be, but it never is."

This Facebook page has about eleven thousand fol-lowers. That seems like a lot of people who care. So why isn't anyone doing anything?

I click on the corporate plan for the new buildings. There's a map of what it will look like. They're basically going to tear down all the old wooden shops. Then they'll build a high-rise hotel and put in new stores.

"See?" Nana Linda points at the map. "The part they want to save—the shops—is only four and a half acres. But the whole project is going to take up more than just Navegando Point—they're going to use up seventy acres."

"That's huge!" I had thought they were just getting rid of the shop area, too. But this is massive. There's an aquarium, but we already have other aquariums—the Birch in La Jolla, SeaWorld, and one in Chula Vista, the south part of the county.

And the entire area where the theater was is gone, too.

I know I should have realized that when Dad and I saw all the shops were closed, but this hits me right in the chest. This means that even if the theater *did* pay more money in rent, the developers were going to kick them out anyway. I guess I thought the stores who paid more money would be able to stay, and that's not true at all. So why would anyone want to pay more, knowing they'd be closed soon no matter what?

That means the cupcake shop isn't going to stay, either.

"That's not right," I say aloud, and Nana Linda pats my shoulder.

Plus, there's no park at all where the peninsula was before, where people could just picnic and hang out. Instead, the old park area is filled with something called *luxury villas*. I point. "What are these?"

Nana Linda peers at it. "I would guess it means places for people to stay. Expensive places right on the water."

"But that means only those people get to see the view!" This seems totally unfair, sort of like if Mom and Dad gave allowance only to one kid even though we all needed the same stuff. I squint at the plan. The only public place is a paved courtyard.

"Big deal." Nana Linda shakes her head. "Just one more place that will cost way too much to go to. You have to pay for parking and all the stores will be expensive."

"It reminds me of Waikiki Beach in Honolulu," Jīchan muses. "You can't see the beach for the hotels."

"Why should the developers be favored?" Nana Linda demands. "This city's in the developers' pockets, I'll tell you that!"

"Calm down," Jīchan says. "You know, those developers helped me get a lot of jobs."

"But you hated working for them," Nana Linda points out.

"We can't stop progress." Jīchan shrugs. "The old Navegando Point is all run-down."

I glare at my grandfather. "Do you mean—blighted?"

"Yeah. It is," he says.

That's just like what they told Dad about his warehouse. I don't know, I'm starting to agree with Nana Linda about this.

"So renovate it!" Nana Linda says.

I can see picket signs dancing in her eyes. "You don't want to, like, chain yourself to the theater or something?"

"That's an idea." She laughs.

"Not again." Jīchan sighs. He disappears into the back bedroom.

"I know." Nana Linda pushes the laptop to me. "How about writing a letter to the Port of San Diego? The port commissioners are in charge of Navegando Point."

"Why don't you do it?" My heart speeds up. I barely want my own teacher to read my writing—why would I want the port people to?

"I'm not the one taking improv there."

I groan. But I know I have no choice. So I start typing, writing the shortest note I can think of.

Dear Port Commissioners,
Why would you take a perfectly good place and make it so yucky on purpose? Please stop immediately.
Sincerely,
Ava Andrews

Nana Linda furrows her brow. "It needs to be more persuasive."

Mr. Sukow would make me change it, too. But this isn't English class, Nana Linda can't give me a bad grade, and I don't feel like working on it anymore. My face flushes as I try to figure out what to say to her that will be a good enough reason for quitting.

Nana Linda looks at me patiently. I think she's going to tell me I'm lazy, but that's more like the kind of thing Luke would say, not her. Then my phone pings, saving me. I grab it. Zelia texted back.

Fosters Freeze is gross anyway.

That's the first time I've ever heard her say that.

Is this Zelia? I type. *Or did a monster steal her phone?*

She doesn't respond.

"Ava," Nana Linda nudges. "Just a quick rewrite."

My stomach feels sour from the ice cream and Zelia's weird text. I want to be done with this. Besides which, there are thousands of grown-ups who haven't done anything to stop the development—I can't make a difference. "Nothing's going to happen if I do write a letter, Nana Linda. I'm only eleven."

"Yet more articulate than most adults."

Yes, and, I hear Miss Gwen saying. What would happen if I said yes?

What if I do my best on this letter and they *still* don't care? It'll be a double failure. It's better not to try. I don't want to *yes, and*. "This is how I want it. This way or nothing." Now all I want to do is hit send. Like throwing a ball of paper into a fire. I doubt they'll read it, anyway.

Jīchan wanders back into the room, pausing to watch us.

Nana Linda squints at me as though I'm speaking Parseltongue. "Just let me edit it."

She's not going to stop unless I say something dramatic. "You're triggering my anxiety now." I want her to leave me alone so I can go into the den and watch my saved TV show.

Nana Linda blinks at me and takes a few seconds before she speaks. "Sweetie. I know you have anxiety, but you can't use that as a shield. In life, sometimes you have to do things that are uncomfortable, or that you don't want to do. Otherwise, you'll never get what you want."

A sharp bolt of shame cuts into me. If only she knew about all my other problems, like running away from Fosters Freeze. What would she say if she knew I didn't want to even tell her about them? I shake my head.

"Maybe Ava just doesn't feel like stirring the pot, Linda," he says to her gently. "She's been working at school all day long. Give her a break."

I nod vigorously. "Yeah."

"Well." She looks at me thoughtfully. "How about we send this to your improv teacher first? Maybe she has some ideas for getting more people involved. There's power in numbers."

This sounds like a good solution to me. Mostly because it means I don't have to worry about it anymore at the moment. "Okay."

"Okay, then." She exchanges a look with my grandfather. "Go watch TV."

Finally. I hop up and run to the den, making sure to give Jīchan a big hug on my way.

CHAPTER 14

The next day, I drag myself over to the ultra-noisy lunch arbor. There are these metal awnings overhead that make the sound bounce off, and there's no way five hundred middle schoolers can eat quietly.

I scan the crowds of kids at the picnic-style tables, hoping someone will wave, and yell, "Ava, over here!" If I see the improv kids, I can sit with them. Tell them about Nana Linda and her making me write a letter.

Maybe they're all hiding from me because of Fosters Freeze. My brain tells me that's probably not true. They probably already have their own lunch routine and aren't even thinking about me. But the little thought won't go away. It's like a tiny crab burrowing into the sand, sinking down into my head and crawling around in there.

"Stop," I say out loud.

"Stop what?" It's Ty, at a table right in front of me. He's spooning some refried beans into his mouth from a recycled cardboard cafeteria tray. He glowers a little and takes a swig of chocolate milk. "I wasn't doing anything."

Not again. I don't know what to say, so I quick-walk away from him, wishing a hole would open itself up so I could hide myself in it. I find a place on the end of a random bench and shove the chicken salad sandwich into my mouth, my ears ringing. The kids next to me keep on eating and talking as if I'm not there.

Every muscle in my body is steel-hard. My shoulders ache and my calf has a charley horse. I move my foot around, trying to loosen it. That happens when I get tense.

I wish Zelia were here. I can't take it anymore. I get out my phone and text her, hiding it under my backpack because we're not supposed to have it on until after school.

Hey.

I can't think of what else to say, so I send that.

To my surprise, the phone pings almost immediately.

Hay is for horses.

This makes me smile a little bit.

I watch more characters appear. *Aren't you at lunch?* Zelia types.

Yeah, but I miss you. She's been weird lately, but I still need her.

Can't talk. At a thing.

I send a smiley face back. My shoulders unclench. Talking to Zelia has always been one of my "coping mechanisms" I have to write on my self-care plan. So just the thought that I'll get to talk to her helps me.

I finish my lunch and go to the blacktop, where other kids scream and run around playing balls, or walk in groups gossiping. I've never been part of a group. Just a duo.

I sit under a tree and get out my journal, but for once in my life, I don't feel like writing. I feel like the Little Mermaid, wanting to be where the people are. Wanting to be something I'm not.

In English class, Cecily doesn't even glance over. Is it because of Fosters Freeze? My stomach cramps thinking about it. Right away, Mr. Sukow gives us a little class time to work on our project. I turn my desk around to face Ty. Ty sticks his legs out straight in front of him, slouching down. He's pretty tall for a sixth-grade boy. His ankles, in thick white athletic socks, stick out beyond his jeans, making him look even taller.

He moves his feet under his desk. "What are you looking at?"

"Nothing." This is going to be just great. I open my Chromebook. "Let's get to work."

We both stare at our own screens. Around us, every-one buzzes with ideas. Are we the only group not getting along? Cecily cackles from the other side of the room—she's working with a boy named Grant. I wish I could be her partner.

"So." Ty seems to read my thoughts, following my sight line over to Cecily. He gets up. "I'm going to ask if we can switch."

I follow him to Mr. Sukow's desk. I'm pretty sure this won't work, but who knows. I kind of admire Ty for trying. Mr. Sukow's sorting some papers and doesn't look up. "Already done?"

I stare at the floor. Ty speaks up. "No, but we want to change partners. This isn't working."

"What about it isn't working?" Mr. Sukow puts down the papers. His face looks like it's been carved out of stone.

"We don't get along."

"You weren't even talking," Mr. Sukow points out. "You didn't try." So he was watching the whole time, not just pretending to work like I thought. Teachers are so sneaky.

Ty lowers his voice and glances back at me. "I just don't want to . . ." He slips into a whisper. "Work with her."

I wish I could melt into a puddle and slip away under the door crack. I didn't do anything. I'm not like one of those kids who doesn't do their share of the work. I listen to my partner. I do all the writing.

If he acted just a little bit nice toward me, we wouldn't have this problem.

"Ava," Mr. Sukow says, "do you feel the same?"

And then I get a hot little flame in my chest, like the one I get when Luke's bugging me. Dad would flip out if I told someone in front of them that I didn't want to work with them.

I shrug.

Ty gives me a *what the heck?* look but I only see it out of the corner of my eye because I'm still mostly staring at the floor. I should have stayed at my desk.

"Nobody's switching." Mr. Sukow folds his hands. "When you enter the workforce, there will be all kinds of people you'll have to learn to get along with. You might as well start now, while the stakes are low."

Ty and I cross our arms at the same time and I try to keep my eyes from rolling out of my head. Low stakes? What does that even mean? That middle school doesn't matter at all?

Mr. Sukow begins his paper-shuffling again. "Go back and try again, please."

We shuffle back to our desks. Ty throws himself into his seat. "I'm going to do research today. Alone."

I nod, but he's already got his back to me, so I'm sure he thinks I'm ignoring him. I should probably say something, but it also seems like it'd be useless to try.

"Hey." Cecily's kneeling beside me. "You want to come

over after school tomorrow and hang out?"

She's not mad at all. Relief makes my insides turn into goo and I almost jump out of my seat. "Yes." And just like that, I forget all about Ty and the assignment.

That evening, I'm washing my face in our bathroom and catch sight of what looks like a big tick bite or something on the side of my nose. Another zit. Not today.

Hudson, like a good older brother, taught me how to squeeze these things. I run a washcloth under hot water, then put it on my pimple until I can't take it anymore. This makes the whitehead show up. Then I take two Q-tips and carefully squeeze.

Mom walks by and stops at the open door. "No! You'll make it scar!"

"It's fine." Will it scar? The thing pops and bleeds, and I press a tissue against it. I take out a Band-Aid and tape it over my nose.

"Do you guys have acne wash in here?" Mom tosses out an empty bottle. "You need to tell me when you run out of stuff."

"I don't use that. It's Luke's." Sharing a bathroom with two brothers is bad in some ways. One, they usually don't clean up after themselves. I guess this could be true with girls and I'm not the cleanest person ever, either, but my brothers have taken it to the next level. But it's good in some ways, too. They don't take long to get ready.

"This bathroom is disgusting." Mom shakes her head. "It's Luke's turn to clean."

I feel a twinge of guilt. Every Saturday, we have to clean before we go do stuff. I was supposed to do it, but I only wiped the counters. The shower and toilet are gross. I couldn't stand to clean them. "Actually, Mom . . . I was supposed to . . ."

Mom doesn't hear. She's grumbling about the luxury of indoor plumbing and how we take everything for granted and no child of hers will be spoiled. I scurry out of there. I'll fix it later.

CHAPTER 15

Cecily lives in a two-story house near the school. She leads me through her living room and kitchen, where a Puerto Rican flag is displayed above the dining table. Wind chimes hang along the patio overhand. It looks like an outdoor living room, with a squishy couch, a ceiling fan, a carpet, and even a TV hanging underneath the patio eave. A big barbecue sits at the other end.

"Wow." I sink into the cushiness. "I've never seen a TV outside before. Except at a restaurant."

"My dad watches football out here a lot." Cecily does a one-shoulder shrug. "You want a soda?" She hops up, opens a refrigerator that's attached to the barbecue, comes back.

"You have an outdoor fridge, too? That's so cool." I accept the can. Lemon-lime. Fine with me. "Are your parents both at work?"

She nods. I open the soda, wondering if my parents would be okay with Cecily's parents not being home. What if something happens? What if there's a fire? Or what if there's an earthquake? Or a robber?

I'm actually allowed to stay home alone, but I don't like it. Not only do I make sure all the doors are locked, sometimes I lock my room and push a chair in front of the door. Just in case.

"Ava? You okay?" Cecily's leaning over. I realize I'm all scrunched up like I'm scared, hugging my knees to my chest, caught up in my anxiety daydream. "My dad gets home at four. That's only an hour."

I nod, forcing my legs down to the floor. "Being alone makes me scared," I admit. My heart thumpity-thumps—I don't usually go around really admitting what I feel. What if Cecily makes fun of me?

She doesn't. "I'm used to it—I'm an only child." She points at the neighbor's house. "Besides, I know everyone on this street, so they'll help me if I need it."

"Oh," I say. I try to imagine a life without my brothers and I can't. "Are you ever lonely?" Zelia's an only child, too, but she and her mom act more like sisters than mother and daughter a lot of the time.

Cecily shrugs. "Nah. I like it."

We sit sipping our soda for a minute, listening to the wind chimes tinkling softly in the breeze. Then Cecily says, "Hey, want to play an improv game?"

I squint at her. "Did you lure me over here just to do improv?"

"Maybe." Cecily grins, and I grin back. "How about Five Things?"

It's a game Miss Gwen taught us. She gave us an object, like *shoebox*. Then we'd have to name five things we'd find in a shoebox. "It doesn't matter what you say," she said. "Just say something. Even a sound. Nothing is wrong."

Of course, my brain wanted to think of the perfect things you could find in a shoebox. I froze. But Ryan spit out, "Jolly Green Giant!"

"One!" we counted with a clap.

"Jolly Ranchers!" Ryan continued.

"Two!" we shouted, clapping again.

"Santa!" Ryan yelled.

"Three!" Clap.

Ryan grabbed his belly. "Ho-ho-ho!"

That made no sense, but nobody minded. "Four!" Clap.

"Coal!" Ryan howled.

"Five!" we screamed and clapped. Then we sang, "Fiiiiii-ve things! These are five things. Five things, five things, five things. THESE ARE FIVE THINGS!" After that, I'd say whatever came into my mouth, even if I was looking at the wall and said, "Wall." Or, "Ummmmm."

It's not the worst game ever. I like that you can say

anything and have it be right. I settle back cross-legged on the couch and nod at Cecily. "Okay."

She gives me the word *barbecue*, I give her *toaster*. Then I get an idea. I smirk at her. "Five things about . . . Mr. Sukow."

Cecily giggles. "Crazy."

I clap. "One."

"Tough."

"Two."

"Smells like lemons."

"Three." I chuckle.

"Secret farter."

"Four." I giggle harder.

"*Chickendog*," she says, and I curl up into a ball, laughing.

"Five," I manage.

We sing the song. "THESE ARE FIVE THINGS!" we shout at the end. I wonder what the neighbors think of us.

Cecily gets up and gathers some small beanbags that are sitting on the coffee table. She walks over to a rectangular plywood box that's got three holes cut in it vertically and tosses one in. "I'm so glad you're in improv. Everyone likes you."

"Really?" An excited little jolt travels over my body. I go over to her and she hands me a beanbag. Normally I would say no thanks because I hate it when people watch me try out new things that I'm bad at, but today it's okay because we're alone. I try to toss it in like she does, but I overshoot it. "I thought . . . I thought everyone might be mad at me for not going to Fosters Freeze." My heart does its thumpity thing, the way it likes to when I'm offering something a little raw.

"Of course not! We just figured you had to go." Cecily laughs, and my heart smooths out its beats.

My hand shakes with relief as I try to throw it in.

"Oh my gosh, you really were worried, weren't you?" She comes over and hugs me, putting her head on my shoulder. "You'd have to do something way worse than that for us to not like you, believe me."

"Like be a stage hog?" We both giggle.

"Exactly."

"Do you know which library they're having improv at yet?" I try the beanbag again. And miss.

She shakes her head. "I wish they'd stop the whole redevelopment."

I stop trying to throw beanbags. "I wrote a letter to the Port of San Diego." I tell her about my nutty Nana Linda and all her activism, and everything I know about Navegando Point.

"I'll do it, too." Cecily busts out her phone and we find the email address to write to the commissioners. Then she taps out a note. *To Whom It May Concern: This is a bad idea.*

"Add in that it's not fair for only the people with money to enjoy the harbor," I say.

She does, then hits send before I can reread any of it. "Done. Now we can get the others to do it, too." Cecily writes out a group text, copying the email address. "We just have to make sure they actually do it. Chad can be kind of lazy about writing." She holds up her phone. "And Ryan says yes, but he says yes to everything and then forgets. Babel definitely will. Jonathan's the wild card."

I pick up the beanbags. When I was with Nana Linda it felt more like writing a fake letter to the Easter Bunny. Now that Cecily's involved, it feels like we're doing something real and important. "Have you known everyone for a long time?"

"Just Ryan and Chad—they went to my elementary school." She hesitates. "Interesting story about Ryan."

I run over and collect the beanbags. "Oh yeah?"

"He used to be the class bully. He was so mean to me. But then his parents put him into improv. I was not happy to see him in class." She squints. "It like . . . calmed him down, I guess. It made him think about other people. And it made me stand up for myself." She shrugs. "He apologized to me. Now we're friends."

I never thought of anyone being able to change. I think of Ty and me. Maybe he needs to do improv. But I'm not going to be the one to suggest it to him.

Does that mean I can change, too? I won't always be this Ava, the one who wants to do stuff but is scared about it. Maybe future Ava will be different.

It's weird to think about. Mind-blowing, like the time I saw Mr. Sukow in a McDonald's and realized teachers actually existed outside the classroom. It was like seeing a dog drive a car or something.

Cecily's phone pings. "They're all in," she reports. She types back, holding it for me to see. *Write it right now, before you forget*, she types.

My eyes fill up for some reason. I wipe the tears off my cheeks. Cecily touches my arm. "What's wrong?"

"I don't know." I shake my head, thinking about why the whole group saying yes to me is affecting me like this. Then I finally get it. "They're all saying *yes, and* to me."

"Sure. We got your back, Ava. That's what a team does." Cecily pulls me into a side hug, and I put my head on her shoulder.

"I never had people doing that for me before," I whisper. "I mean, besides my family. And excluding Luke." This is the first real team I've ever been on. I didn't know it could be like this. Other people supporting me, with pretty much no questions asked.

"Well, you do now. So don't worry, Ava."

People say that to me all the time when my anxiety ramps up. For probably the first time in my life, I do stop worrying. At least for now. "Thanks."

Cecily's phone pings.

Email sent! Ryan says.

"That was fast!" I peer at the screen.

"They promised to do it right away." Cecily hands me her phone while she tosses more beanbags.

Done! Done! Done! The rest of them reply.

"Wow," I say. "That's amazing."

Cecily takes the phone back. "Your turn."

These emails could be the thing that will actually change the Brancusi Group's mind. I toss the beanbag again. Finally, once, I throw it kind of right, and it slips into the hole. "I did it!" We high-five each other.

CHAPTER 16

My happiness only lasts for two seconds once I get home. Luke's standing outside my room, arms crossed. "I've been waiting for you."

Now why is he mad? What did I do wrong? My heart does a weird hummingbird thing. "Because I took your extra pencil lead? I'm sorry. I ran out."

"You took my pencil lead? Ava!" he sputters. "Okay. That's another issue. But this is why I've been waiting." He bends over, picks up a bunch of cleaning products, thrusts them into my hands. "For you to clean the bathroom the way you were supposed to last week. I'm not picking up your slack. Even though I didn't call you out on it the way I should have." Luke nods. "You can thank me for not getting you into trouble with Mom."

Fair enough. I wouldn't have blamed him if he'd told. "Thanks," I say. "I'm sorry I didn't clean the bathroom right. But maybe you guys could help keep it clean in between?"

"If you fish all your hair out of the drain," he says. "We're all responsible for the mess."

I sigh. I guess he's right. I go into our disgusting bathroom and open the window.

Later that afternoon, I get settled in the reading space Dad made for me by the window. I always wanted a window seat, but there wasn't enough room to build one in my tiny space, so he got me this upholstered bench with bookcases on either side and lots of pillows. It's my fake window seat.

The window faces the back patio, which is both good and bad. Good when nobody's out there. Bad when my parents have friends over late at night.

I also like it because there's a tree outside that Jīchan and Bāchan gave us when we moved in. Or so I'm told—I wasn't born yet. But when my parents bought the house, back when Luke was little, they came over with a flowering orchid tree. It has large hot-pink flowers. Mom calls it a dragonflower tree. I like to stare at it while I'm thinking.

My grandparents have one, too. Mom says it was my grandmother's favorite tree because the hummingbirds love it and she loved hummingbirds. There are always a few that come around, dipping their needle-beaks into the blooms, their wings ablur and their feathers gleaming red and green.

I saw one stop once, going so still I thought it had

died. Mom said they go into a "torpor state" when they sleep, so completely motionless it's hard to tell if it's alive. "How do you tell?" I'd asked her.

"If they get up in twenty minutes or so, they're alive. Otherwise, they're not."

One buzzes by the window now, but it doesn't stop. It looks in at me and I wave. It's probably looking at its own reflection, to be honest.

I lean my phone against the ICD monitor machine I have on my nightstand. There's a person symbol, a phone symbol, and a doctor symbol. Every few months, the ICD sends a report to the doctor and tells them if the device is working right and whether I've had any issues. If I have an "incident," as Dr. White, my cardiologist, calls them, I'm supposed to hit the button above the phone. That sends him a transmission.

It actually makes me feel more secure. If my device doesn't work right, they'll know about it right away. And it does make a handy nightlight, with the glow from the symbols on it. I open up my English journal for the first time since Mr. Sukow shared it. I read it over and chuckle a few times. It's not the worst thing I ever wrote. I don't know why I was afraid to have anyone read it.

"I *am* a writer," I say. It sounds weird out loud.

I think about the Five Things game Cecily and I played. Now, on my blank page, I write, *These are five things you'd find in . . . Ava.*

Daydreaming. One.

Ice cream. Two.

ICD. Three.

Anxiety. Four.

Writing. Five.

I sing the song in my head. *THESE ARE FIVE THINGS!* I write in big block letters. Yes. These are me.

I'm kind of surprised that none of them are negative. I guess maybe anxiety is, but that's also just a part of me. Like my arm. Or my ICD.

Then, because I'm avoiding working on the napkin project, among other homework things, I start looking up things to do in Maine. Blueberry picking, yes. Lobster fishing—probably not. Lobster eating—yes. I've never had a lobster, but that seems like a thing people do there.

A knock on my door surprises me. Everyone in my family has a unique knock. This one's regular. "Who is it?" I close my journal.

"Nana Linda," a muffled voice says.

I cringe as I glance around my room at the socks and pajamas I should have picked up earlier. I'm slacking on my chores. Well, that's nothing new. I seem to leave a trail of stuff wherever I go, without meaning to. I kick a sock and a pair of underwear under the bed. "Um, come in!"

Nana Linda opens the door. She doesn't seem to notice the mess. "Hey, Ava. Jīchan and I are on the way out to dinner at the Sweet Salad Buffet, so I wanted to see if anyone wants to come." She sits down on the floor, tossing aside a sock without making a face like I would have, and leans forward so her elbows are resting on the floor.

I do like the Sweet Salad and their all-you-can-eat soups and salads and muffins. I look at my Chromebook, wishing I'd done my homework instead of thinking about Maine and stuff. "I want to, but I've got this English project I'm working on." I sit next to her and imitate the pose. "Hey, my friend and I made the whole improv team write to Navegando Point."

She chuckles. "*Made* them?"

"Convinced them."

"Wonderful! That's the hardest part, getting people to do something. Unless there's a huge public outcry, the developers will just proceed as normal. And it seems like nobody who lives in San Diego really cares about a touristy place like Navegando Point. Or if they do, they're not speaking up." She bends her head low so her face is hidden. "Ugh. I sat too long today and I'm all sore."

"But, Nana Linda—there's a public meeting. What about that?" I tell her what I heard. Nana Linda straightens and looks it up on her phone.

"Ah-ha!" She nods. "It's tomorrow night."

"They didn't give much notice—like less than two weeks?" I shake my head.

"That's a common tactic. They wait until it's almost too late for people to organize. Though they probably did advertise it somewhere—just not anywhere people could see." She brushes back her hair.

My heart thumps, but it's not anxiety I'm feeling. It's something different. The same thing I feel when people cheat at video games or things like that.

Navegando Point is basically going to close right in front of us unless we do something. Nana Linda was right. We do need to try. Dad always says that if you do nothing, nothing will happen. "One hundred percent of zero is zero," Dad likes to say. "Better to at least try."

"I want to go," I say, surprising myself. I wait for the anxiety again.

Nothing. My palms are a little sweaty, but that's it. "I won't have to talk, will I?" I ask her.

"I'll talk this time." She smiles at me, tousles my hair. "But I want your help. We need to get people to care."

Once again, I wish Zelia were here. She'd be full of ideas. "There's a cemetery full of Spanish sailors underneath Navegando Point," I say. "Will people care about that?"

"I don't think so because there's already a historical plaque." Nana Linda sticks her leg out into another stretch.

I deflate like an accordion. "Oh." That was the most interesting historical thing about Navegando Point.

"Sorry, but let's think about what people care about besides historical stuff."

What do I care about? My family. My friends. My

house. My school. My community.

"People should care about Navegando Point," I say slowly, "because it should belong to everyone. And it seems like there aren't many places like that anymore."

"Bingo!" Nana Linda acts like this is the answer she's been waiting for. "It's called gentrification. That's when an area gets redeveloped with more expensive real estate and prices out the people who used to live there or use it."

"Like what happened with Dad's Cotillion and all those businesses," I say. The unfairness of that hits me again. Maybe some progress can't be helped, but can't they do it so they don't just kick everyone out?

She stretches her arms. "So. Step one. We go to the Port of San Diego public hearing. See what they have to say when we point this out. Then make our plan based on what happens. Who knows, maybe they'll see it our way."

I like plans, I realize. Just having one about the theater makes me feel like I'm doing something. Like there's at least a *possibility* of some good thing. And it's a lot better than doing nothing all the time. I smile at Nana Linda. "Can we do corpse pose?" That's my favorite because all you have to do is lie there.

"Only if you don't let me fall asleep." She lies on her back, with me beside her, our hands at our sides. Just breathing in and out.

* * *

After Nana Linda leaves, I FaceTime Zelia. I haven't talked to her since she showed me her pink-and-blue hair and put down improv. Just the texts. I've been hoping she'd realize she was wrong and call me and apologize. But that never happened.

I decide to be mature and move past it. I mean, we've texted since then. She answered me, even though she was weird about Fosters Freeze. She might have been trying to make me feel better. Dad always says we should assume people mean no harm until proven otherwise— another Cotillion lesson. Besides, I want to know what she thinks.

She answers, sticking her face too close to the camera. "Hey."

"Hi." My heart skips a little, and suddenly I'm a little shaky. Like my body thinks she'll say something else about improv. "How's it going?"

"Ugh. Lots of homework. I can't talk long." She moves away from the camera so I can see her book-covered bed. "I'm going to be up until ten."

"I'm sorry." Now I feel kind of bad for calling.

"So what's up?" She scratches her nose.

"I . . . I wanted to ask you something about . . . about . . ." I hate how my voice is suddenly small and stammering. I swallow.

"About what?" She's writing something in a notebook.

Suddenly I don't want to risk making her mad. And I realize I don't know what to say because who would have predicted improv would make Zelia mad? "What did you think about the new She-Ra episodes?" I ask her instead because we used to watch that together.

Zelia sets down her pen. "Oh, I loved them! Did you see . . ."

And then, finally, we have a nice conversation. Though I didn't get to talk about what was really on my mind. *It's fine*, I tell myself. Maybe we're at the stage of our friendship where we just talk about TV shows and weather and never anything important.

After we hang up, I have to press the heels of my hands into my eyes so I don't tear up. I miss Zelia so much. The old Zelia, who I could talk to about anything in the world. What happened to her? I take out the notebook I use for sketching.

Close. One.

Sisters. Two.

Far. Three.

Hurt. Four.

Alone. Five.

These are five things.

These are five things about me and Zelia.

I close the notebook and put it under my pillow.

CHAPTER 17

The next day, I wait for Ty at lunch. The jacaranda tree by the arbor smells like sweet and spicy peppers, the purple flowers floating above our heads in clouds. Jīchan says that Washington, DC, and Japan have cherry blossoms; we have jacarandas. And the blooms last longer. I settle myself under it, perched on the edge of the calf-high concrete planter, trying to relax.

Ty walks up, clutching a cafeteria tray with a quesadilla, rice, and canned peaches on it, his shoulders hunched and his sandy-brown hair falling over one eye. As he approaches, my body starts to squinch up, too, like it's reacting to his *I don't want to be here* vibes.

Maybe I'd rather not be here, either, but at least I have the good manners not to show it. Then I smile because that sounds like something Dad would say. And then I frown because that means I'm actually learning something at Cotillion, which is kind of against my whole argument for not going. Anyway, it's about considering other people's feelings.

Which is also sort of like improv. You can't just do what you personally want all the time, as if nobody else is important.

As I'm thinking all this, Ty kind of glares down at me. "I can't believe I still have to work with you."

Hello to you, too, I say in my head, and my blood freezes up again. He already doesn't like me, so anything I say can and will be held against me. Instead of answering, I shrug and avoid his eyes. When I'm quiet and look people in the eye, they sometimes get mad, act like I'm challenging them. Hudson says that's because gorillas do it and humans are still basically primates.

I sit down cross-legged on the concrete and open the Chromebook on my lap.

"This is the most useless assignment ever," Ty declares.

That's what I think, too, but I don't say so because I'm too jammed up inside. Besides, if I agree with Ty, he'll disagree just to be contrary. Sort of like Luke. "Where's your Chromebook?" I look around.

Ty sits down next to me, balancing his food tray. "It got soda on it."

Oh. That's not good. Ty will have to pay for that. Or his parents will.

"Let's get this over with." He nods at me. "You want

136

to type or do you want me to?"

I open the laptop. Obviously I'll type. I don't want him spilling stuff on my equipment. And I definitely don't trust that chocolate milk, which comes in a plastic bag thing.

"So we have the napkin. What do we like about the napkin?" Ty says. "It's, uh, paper. It's a square."

Paper. Square. I type these words. *Absorbent. Need them when you eat messy foods, like ribs and ice cream.*

When I look up, Ty's staring at me intently. He's so close to me I can see flecks of brown in his blue eyes. "Are you not going to say anything?" he says.

At this pressure, my words curdle and crumble. I turn the screen so he can see what I typed. He glances at it, nods. "Good for the planet?" he adds.

"Are they?" I automatically say, and he glowers. Was I supposed to accept that? I type it in. "I mean, cloth might be better."

"But you have to wash the cloth ones and use water." He holds up the napkin. "This is recycled."

You have to cut down trees to make paper, and you need water to grow the trees, I almost tell him. I don't know which is better, now that he says that. We can research later.

Ty pulls a small white paper bag out of his backpack. My nose recognizes it before I see it. He opens it and removes a chocolate cupcake.

"Hey." Cecily's here. "Whatcha doing?"

"We're painting a fence. What does it look like we're doing?" Ty says this lightly, not as annoyed with Cecily as he is with me, and she grins.

"I brought paint. I'll join you." She mimes using a paintbrush.

Ty's standing, empty tray in hand. "Well, I'm done. I'm going to play some kickball."

What? He's already leaving? I shake my head. But we haven't gotten to really work on the script. *Let's just do this thing already*, I want to say, but by the time I form the words, Ty's disappeared across the lunch arbor.

"Sheesh." Cecily tears open her Lunchable. "Did you steal his precious ring or something?" She launches into a Gollum impression. *"Precious. My precious."*

I giggle. "I wish." I shrug. "I don't know." I chew my bottom lip. I hope Mr. Sukow gives us class time to do this. We're working on other units, too, not just these projects. I don't want to give up any more of my free time to Ty. Maybe I'll just do it all myself, and Ty can put his name on it.

That's it, I decide. That's exactly what I'll do.

Cecily and I keep talking all through lunch. When the bell rings, I realize two things. I haven't thought of Zelia once.

And hanging out with a new person no longer feels like the first day of middle school.

CHAPTER 18

I'm in my room trying to do homework. Nana Linda will be here in a half hour to take me to the developer community meeting. I don't want to think about that, though, because thinking about that makes my armpits sweat.

Luckily—or unluckily, I guess—I'm having enough trouble with this project that I can't think about the meeting. This advertising assignment is obviously cursed. Not only do I have to deal with Ty, I'm now having a ton of technical difficulties. The app's frozen. I restart the Chromebook. The thing whirs and whines—it's probably about to die. One more awesome thing to happen.

In the kitchen I hear Mom and Dad clinking around, doing dishes after dinner and chatting in low voices. Sometimes I hear Mom giggle and I know Dad's probably kissing her or something. Ew. But I remind myself that I'm lucky. Zelia told me that she loved watching my parents together. Hers got divorced years ago and she barely sees her father. "You'd rather have them kiss than fight, wouldn't you?" she said once when I complained about their caramel-level gooeyness. That made me change my viewpoint.

Zelia can always do that for me.

While I wait for this thing to reboot, I try calling and texting Zelia. I want to talk to her, tell her about my problem with Ty. Our conversation got so weird so fast last time.

But she doesn't answer. I try not to worry about whether Zelia's in a coma on top of everything else. If something was wrong with her, her mother would have told us.

I think about texting Cecily, but I barely know her. I mean, I went to her house, but is she going to care about my problems? What if she thinks I'm a weirdo for telling her my secrets? Right now she thinks I'm pretty cool. I don't want to mess that up.

I better not say anything.

"Ugh," I groan out loud. When it finally opens again, my file is nowhere to be seen.

"Crud." I look all over the folders for it. Nothing. I do a search.

It's like it never existed. Luckily, it's after dinner and Hudson's home. I go knock on the boys' door, my Chromebook in hand.

Luke flings it open. "What do you want?" He doesn't bother to take out an earbud. He and Hudson have rules that if they're both home, they listen to music on their phones instead of playing it on speakers. Luke's music is so loud I can hear it when the headphones are inside his ears. Once again, he hasn't showered yet after soccer, and he smells like grass and a hundred teenage boys.

I wrinkle my nose. "You're going to go deaf."

"What?" Luke says, leaning forward with his hand cupped around his ear.

"I said, you're going to go deaf!" But then I see him laughing. That joke is never funny no matter how many times he does it. I roll my eyes. "Is Hudson in there?"

Luke acts like he's going to keep blocking me with his body, but then his phone buzzes and he turns to get it off his desk. I leap in.

Hudson's sprawled out on the bottom bunk, books and papers everywhere, a giant pair of bright green headphones over his ears. Somehow out of this chaos, a straight-A average will emerge. No matter how late he has to stay up, Hudson will get it done. Sometimes Dad has to come take books out of his room so Hudson will go to sleep.

I'm not looking forward to high school. I don't think I can work that much. Just thinking about it turns my armpits into geysers.

Hudson takes off his headphones. "Almond?" He offers

me a small bowl. He eats them every two hours to keep his blood sugar stable, he says, and his brain working.

I take one, even though they're unsalted and taste like cardboard. Not that I've ever had cardboard. "I need help." I feel bad for asking, seeing all his homework, but Hudson nods and pushes his laptop aside and pats the quilt. On Hudson's wall, over his bed, he's tacked up lots of photos of him dancing. Him in New York last summer. Him with all his friends.

The boys have a desk at one end of the loft bed, and another against the wall. They only sit at their desks to play computer games and store junk, as far as I can tell. Luke climbs back on his bed, his phone in hand, texting someone. "Who are you talking to?" I ask.

"None of your beeswax," Luke says.

Hudson waves to me. "Let me see your Chromebook, Ava." First Hudson tries fixing the program, digging around in the memory and files. "This a free app?" He sighs. "I think it ate your project."

A fluttery feeling rises. "Can't we get it back?"

"I'm going to email the developer." He shakes his head. "Just write it on paper."

"But Ty and I used the app!" I cry out.

"I'm sorry, Ava." Hudson taps out an email. "That's the problem with free apps. They're buggy. But maybe the developer has a way of retrieving it."

Luke taps away on his phone. "Mr. Sukow is super

picky about doing it his way. You should redo it in that app."

"Then you help her. Make sure it's getting saved right." Hudson pushes the Chromebook toward him.

"I don't have time." Luke texts away.

"You have time to text, but not to help your own sister?" Hudson makes a grab for Luke's phone, but Luke holds it out of the way.

I get a panicky feeling, the way I always do when this stupid equipment fails. Some new problem comes up all the time—no internet connection, printer won't work, can't sign in to the school system. I wish all my classes used paper and pencil.

The project's not due for a few more weeks, but I'm still worried. Occasionally my anxiety makes me slow and gummed up, so my 504 plan says I can ask for extra help and get extra time. But I hate doing it. It's like admitting I'm an idiot or something, even though I know that's not true.

Sometimes when I ask, I can see the teachers thinking, *Why does she need extra time for such a simple project?* Like last year, I needed more time to finish a book report mobile. I was so worried about messing it up that I had a hard time starting, until before I knew it was due, and Dad made me ask my teacher. Everyone else in the class did it on time.

I'm afraid Mr. Sukow will think I'm not smart. He

told me my writing's hilarious, so this project has to be really good, too, or he'll be disappointed. The whole class will think, *That Ava's a one-hit wonder.*

Luke taps away on the keyboard. "It's simple, Ava. Did you save it like this?" He shows me.

"I save stuff on Google Drive all the time. I'm not stupid, Luke."

"I didn't say you were."

"You pretty much did," I say. "Your tone."

"I have no tone." Luke taps around some more. "Just redo it."

I shake my head, frustrated tears already starting. "I don't remember all our words." Ty's going to hate me. He'll blame me, even though it's not my fault.

"Stop whining." Luke puts down the Chromebook. "Why should I help you if you're not even going to try?"

The room starts going blurry. I rub my temples, my breath hot and fast in my throat. "I am trying." In my chest comes that strange, heavy feeling. No hummingbird this time. More like a raven.

"Then email Mr. Sukow!" Luke explodes. "What's the big deal?"

My chin drops to my chest.

"Cut that out." Hudson frowns at Luke. "You're stressing her. That's not helpful."

"Well, she's got to learn how to deal with the real world sometime," Luke argues. Luke hardly ever argues with Hudson. Maybe it's because Hudson's still a head taller than Luke, or maybe it's because Hudson's always been our leader, the one who made sure neither of us got hit by cars when we crossed streets or went through parking lots. "Otherwise she'll just fail at everything in life! She won't even try to solve her problems."

Hudson smacks his laptop closed. "You don't have to be a jerk about it."

"She's always trying to get out of work." Luke points at me. "Like the bathroom. I got in trouble for that, not her. Mom yelled at me."

"I highly doubt Mom *yelled* at you about the bathroom," Hudson says in his most high-and-mighty voice. "The only time I've ever heard Mom yell at you is when you ran into the street after a ball when you were four. And that was to get you to stop."

Luke stands and kicks the side of Hudson's mattress. "You always take her side."

What Luke's saying is all true. Hudson does always take my side. I did mess up the bathroom thing. I *do* try to get out of things, like rewriting that letter for the Port of San Diego and figuring out this program. I *am* going to fail at everything in my life. My crying starts for real now, big fat tears streaming out of my eyes, and it's hard to breathe.

"Go take a walk," Hudson tells Luke, and Luke stomps out. My oldest brother puts his arm around my shoulders. "Ava, don't worry. It's only homework."

He knows saying *don't worry* doesn't work. It's like telling the sun not to set. I lean into him and sob, and feel stupid for crying. Hudson doesn't understand how it is to work with Ty. It feels like my whole future depends on this one assignment.

I leave their bedroom and run down to my bedroom. I can barely breathe, and I hope it's because of the tears and not my heart. It thumpity-thumps, and my chest feels hot.

I look at my ICD pacemaker monitor, at the picture of the doctor. Should I press it? Is this an event? No. It'll pass. Besides, if I press it, the doctors will charge us money, for looking at the report. Instead, I blow my nose until it's dry, and lie back on my bed.

"These are five things," I say out loud, to distract myself. My voice sounds weird all alone in my room. I don't really ever talk when I'm alone. I change out of my grungy sweats into some slightly nicer jeans. "These are five things about . . . Luke. *Stinky.* One!" My voice is quiet. I imagine Miss Gwen telling us, *Louder! Faster!* so I shout the count back to myself like someone else said the word. "*Stubborn.* Two! *Know-it-all.* Three! *Mean.* Four! *Ridiculous.* Five!" I scream at the end. "Five things. *These are five things!*"

"Are you talking about me?" Luke yells from down the hall.

"Not everything is about you, Luke! Sheesh!"

In a little bit, I feel better. I get up and wash my face and brush my hair. It's almost time for Nana Linda to pick me up for the meeting. I look at myself in the mirror. My skin's a little red, but it's not bad. No one can tell I've been crying.

Maybe that's what I was really being upset about—having to go to this meeting. I shake my body like I saw Miss Gwen do, top to bottom. "You can do this, Ava." I nod at my reflection.

"Who are you talking to?" Luke asks from outside the door.

I open it and push past him. "To Ava Andrews."

"Improv's making you weird," he calls after me.

The doorbell rings and I go to answer it. Nana Linda stands on the porch step, dressed in a black tunic and leggings with a black knit scarf laced with gold thread on top. "Ready?"

I close the door. "As ready as I'll ever be."

The meeting's in a room in one of the Navegando Point restaurants called the Fish Place. There are about a dozen chairs set up in front of a podium, and I count just five people besides the five Brancusi Group workers. I've never seen any of them before, and they're all ages and genders. They amble over to the coffee and pour themselves some. Maybe they're just here for the coffee.

I spot Brett Rosselin with four of her coworkers. "Welcome," she's saying. "Welcome, welcome." She gives me a bright smile and I get the feeling that a robot is smiling at me.

I wonder if she read our emails. I want to ask, but to be honest, Brett Rosselin kind of scares me. She definitely would play a villain in a movie.

Nana Linda will ask her during the meeting. I don't have to do anything. I clutch Nana Linda's hand as we move around the room. They have a model of the new plan on a table. It's like a miniature village, all laid out under Plexiglas. There are even tiny people walking along the water.

My heart drops. It looks even worse as a model than it does as a drawing.

"We are committed to keeping our existing Navegando Point businesses running while adding new ones," Brett Rosselin says. She sounds like one of those TV people who speak up for the president and people like that. Shiny and tinny.

Lie, I want to shout. What about the ones that are already closed? What about the improv theater? Nana Linda raises her hand as if she's had the same question.

"No comments until the end," Brett Rosselin says. "For those members of the public who signed up to speak before the meeting." She blinks at Nana Linda with her fake smile. "Did you sign up?"

Before the meeting started? I'm pretty sure Nana Linda didn't sign up for anything—we came in and sat down. Nobody said anything. She stiffens. "No," she says.

I look around at the bored-looking people sipping their coffees and checking their phones. There are just five other "members of the public" here. Who signed up?

"Lip service," Nana Linda mutters. Then, louder, "How are you going to do that when half of the stores are closed?"

"Ma'am, we're going to have to ask you to leave," the man says.

"I'll answer that. Those businesses chose to leave rather than renegotiate. Believe me, we tried to work things out." Brett blinks rapidly. "We are committed to helping local businesses."

I wonder if someone wrote that down for her to say over and over.

Nana Linda stands now. "Can anyone here vouch for that?" She addresses Brett. "Or do you have documentation of how you're helping the fifty local, family-owned businesses in Navegando Point?"

I want to stop this whole meeting, but I can't. They wouldn't listen to me anyway. My fingers grip the sides of my chair. I'm just praying that it turns out all right.

The man starts walking toward her. Nana Linda picks up her bag. "Fine, fine." We walk out. She puts her arm around me.

I don't know whether to be mad or proud of her. That took some guts. I've never seen anyone interrupt a meeting like that. "Why couldn't you wait until the end?"

"Because they weren't going to let me talk." Nana Linda pulls me into her, and I put my arm around her. She probably needs a hug right now as much as I do. "Sometimes speaking up means doing things differently."

I squeeze her. "What now?"

"There's plenty more to do, Ava. An online petition. Letter writing. Calls. All kinds of things." She sighs. "We just have to get people fired up enough to participate."

We didn't even find out if they read the letters. If I'd asked Brett before the meeting, then she might have been forced to answer me. I'm let down, the way I was when Dad promised us a trip to Disneyland and then Hudson got a sore throat. There has to be something else we can do. This can't be the end, with Brett Rosselin and the Brancusi Group winning and Navegando Point being torn down without anyone saying another word. That's not the way stories finish.

Is it?

CHAPTER 19

On the way home, I send a group text to the improv group telling them what happened. Cecily writes back: *That's awful—anybody wanna meet tomorrow and talk about what to do?*

But what *can* we do? I tug on Nana Linda's sleeve. "Hey, Nana Linda, would it be okay if my improv group came to your house tomorrow so we can . . . you know?" I punch the air. "Figure out what to do next." *And I'll get to hang out with them,* I add in my head. Which I like.

She squeezes my hand. "Of course. The more the merrier."

I squeeze her hand back.

Mr. Sukow gives us class time to work on our group project the next day. Sometimes thinking about it makes my stomach hurt and then I don't even want to try to do it, so I don't. Ty's got his desk pushed against mine, but his head is lowered, his face hidden by the Chromebook cover and the black hoodie. He kind of stinks the way my brothers stink when they don't shower and don't open their bedroom window all weekend. I wrinkle my nose.

Of course that's when he looks up and sees me. My look of grossed-out-ness. I cringe, feeling my face go hot. "What's your problem?" he says. "I'm just trying to fix what you lost."

"The program lost it. Not me." The woman who wrote the app had written back to us, apologizing, but hadn't been able to recover my document. Mr. Sukow said we could have an extra week to make up for it if we wanted. Both of us said no. We don't want to work on this a second longer than necessary.

"You should have made a backup in Word. You were the typist."

I shake my head. He sounds like Luke. "Are we going to talk about this forever?" *Or can you build a time machine to travel into the past to fix it?* I add in my head.

Ty cranks his neck back to look at me, startled by the gush of words. "Fine."

"Fine."

Ty's words appear on my screen in our shared document.

This is a napkin. It is absorbent. It helps you clean up spills. Buy me.

I blink at him. It's not long enough. It's boring. It's

never going to convince anyone to buy a napkin. But he's smirking at me as if he's written the best thing on the planet. Just like when Luke sets the dining table and doesn't bother folding the napkins.

I add, *Made from 100% recycled materials, Bliss Napkins are the best on earth.*

"Bliss? What's that?" Ty wrinkles his nose like I just ate brussels sprouts and had a stinky toot.

I smile and point at my mouth. "Happy."

Ty deletes the word and types *happy*. "Too fancy."

"It's not." Is he really going to do this to me? *Bliss*, I type back.

Blis| I watch the backspace get rid of my word.

Bliss bliss

Blissbliss

bliss

bliss

I type over and over again.

HAAPPPPPY, he types. Yelling.

I'm about to unleash about three hundred *bliss*es when something soft yet rough hits my forehead and bounces down into my lap.

The napkin.

"Did you throw this at me?" My heart's beating fast and my chest burns. I glare at Ty and uncrumple it as best I can. "We need this."

"I give up." Ty gets up and stalks over to Mr. Sukow.

"I can't work with her, Mr. Sukow."

I follow. "Mr. Sukow, Ty . . ."

"Mr. Sukow, Ava . . ." Ty says.

Mr. Sukow holds up his hand. "You're both talking at the same time. Ava, you first."

"Figures," Ty grumbles.

My chest feels like I ate too much hot salsa. "He threw something at me!" Is my heart doing okay? My fingers go up to my neck, looking for my pulse. It's pounding hard.

"Just a napkin!" Ty raises his voice. "She's impossible."

The burning sensation goes away and my heart stops pounding. I think I got paced, but I'm not sure. Anyway, I'm okay, I remind myself.

My head hurts.

"All right." Mr. Sukow gets eerily calm, the same way Dad does when he's about to deliver justice. "I have thirty-five other students who need my attention, and frankly I'm tired of both your attitudes. Why don't you go down to the office and talk to Ms. Shepherd?"

My palms go cold. "Ms. Shepherd?" That's the vice principal. Luke calls her "Bad Cop" because she's the school disciplinarian.

Mr. Sukow picks up his school phone. "Go on."

Ty and I walk down the hallway, Ty in front of me. The heels of his sneakers are worn down at the corners and there are holes near the rubber. I don't know why boys always let their shoes get so bad. Last year, Luke didn't tell Mom he needed new shoes until the sole fell off on the way to Disneyland.

If Zelia were here, I wouldn't be in this mess at all because she would be the one who stuck up for me. She would probably be here now. She definitely would have told me what to do. Once, I had to do an assignment with a girl in fourth grade and she took over the whole thing. Zelia told me to just let her. "Who cares?" she'd said. "She can do all the work if she's going to be like that." And I'd gone along with it.

I follow Ty into the office through the maze of desks. The receptionist is an older lady with hair dyed almost egg-yolk yellow, curled closely against her head. She wears a sweatshirt with a wolf howling at the moon on it. Hudson has the same sweatshirt, but he says he wears his *ironically*. She's got all kinds of wolf pictures tacked up around her cubicle, though, so I guess she really likes wolves. "Hello again, Tyler." She squints at me. "And you are?"

"Ava." I guess she knows Ty by name even though school only started a few weeks ago.

Ty flops into a wooden chair. I sit, my stomach switching between feeling like it's boiling and like there's a block of ice in it. I've never been in trouble in my entire life. I'm like the anti-trouble kid. The only thing teachers have to say about my behavior is that I could speak up more.

"My mom can't come in," Ty informs the receptionist. "She's working." He twists his mouth. "She just lost one of her jobs, so she can't leave."

His mom had two jobs? "My mom's working, too," I say quietly. My dad will be the one who comes in. And he won't be happy. I swallow.

"Well, if my mom leaves work early, she doesn't get paid." Ty chews on a fingernail. "She might even get fired."

"Then I guess you'd better stop getting into trouble, huh?" The receptionist smiles in a teeth-baring kind of way.

Ty doesn't react, but her words send a shudder over my skin, as if a bunch of spiders have run across my shoulders. I go as still as possible, as if she won't be able to see me.

The phone buzzes and the receptionist picks up. "Okay, Tyler, Ms. Shepherd's ready for you."

I'm sweating so hard my shirt sticks to my back. My pants, too. My breath is kind of fast. I don't know whether I'm going to pass out or barf.

I lean forward and wrap my arms around my thighs. "I feel sick," I say truthfully.

The receptionist comes over and feels my forehead because obviously she thinks I'm making it up. "Clammy. Let's get you to the nurse."

* * *

The nurse, Mrs. Romero, knows who I am—she knows all the kids with medical plans. She takes one look at me and decides I don't have to see Ms. Shepherd in her office. "You're having a little anxiety attack," she tells me. Instead she has me lie on the cot, lined with paper, in the dark and cool room. "Just relax and you'll be fine."

Ty's not going to be happy. He'll say I'm getting special treatment again. And he might be kind of right. Who else gets sent to the office and ends up lying down?

I'm having an anxiety attack, which means I need to calm myself somehow. If I don't, my heart won't like the stress.

Oh no.

I try to notice my surroundings. White walls. Weird disinfectant smell that reminds me of the hospital. Which reminds me of being sick. Which reminds me that my heart could be going nuts.

I turn over on my side to face the wall, paper crinkling under me. Sometimes I wonder what it would be like if I had been born into another body, a healthy one that could dance and play soccer without thinking about what might happen.

I take a shaky breath. I need to think about something else. *Five things about improv.*

Laughing. One.

Miss Gwen. Two.

Cecily. Three.

Happy. Four.

IKEA. Five.

Okay, IKEA has nothing to do with improv but that's what popped into my head, and there are no wrong answers. "These are five things," I say out loud, and then my stomach growls as I remember Swedish meatballs.

In a little while, a woman comes in. Ms. Shepherd, the vice principal. She's tall, with an Afro that frames her face like a halo. She sits on a chair next to me. "You feeling any better, Ava?"

I nod. I didn't know she knew who I was.

"I had a talk with Ty and Mr. Sukow," she says. "I know you want to switch partners but I really think this is a good chance for you and Ty to work it out."

That's what Mr. Sukow says. That's probably what everyone who's over the age of fourteen would say. My parents included. I sit up. "Did you call my parents?"

"You don't have a temperature, and you didn't throw up, so no," Ms. Shepherd says. "Did you want me to?"

I'd meant because of the other thing. The in-trouble thing. I sure don't want my parents to know about that. It's just totally embarrassing. "No."

"Okay, then." Ms. Shepherd pats my arm. "Well, you and Ty just have to do some give-and-take. Communicate instead of argue. If you have another problem, go to Mr. Sukow. Okay?"

I nod, my neck hot. "I'm sorry."

"I know you are. You're a good student." Ms. Shepherd stands. "I'm glad it's all worked out." She walks away, shutting the door behind her. I wonder what adults consider "worked out" because nothing feels worked out to me at all, and I don't know what I'm supposed to do next. So I just lie on the cot, waiting for someone to tell me what to do.

CHAPTER 20

It's less than a half mile to my grandparents' house from school. Usually that feels like a somewhat longish walk, but today it doesn't. Chad and Ryan and Cecily and I are like a jumble of puppies milling around on the sidewalk, jumping on lawns, zooming around.

"I think it was really rude of Ty to ask to be switched, right in front of you," Cecily tells me. "It's like, dude, just deal." She takes my arm.

"Right?" I lean into her. Just her saying that makes me feel a thousand times better. At least for now, until I have to deal with Ty again.

Ryan walks backward. "I don't know what he's complaining about. I'd be your project partner anytime." He trips on a crack and catches himself.

"Me too." Chad's galloping sideways in the street gutter.

We pass by a cute little blue house with a *FOR SALE*

sign in front of it. Cecily grabs a flyer, looks at the price, and shrieks. She shoves it at me. "Two bedrooms and it's seven hundred thousand dollars!"

My heart drops. I knew houses were expensive here, but I never looked at how much. "I'm not going to be able to afford to live here when I grow up."

"My plan is to marry a rich old lady." Chad flaps his arm like a chicken. "Then I'll never have to get a job."

"That's a terrible plan," Ryan says.

Chad rolls his eyes. "Dude, I'm not being serious. Obviously. My plan A is to be a bank robber."

"Maybe things will change by the time we're grown-ups," Cecily offers.

"We'll probably all have to move out of state if we want to afford to, like, live," Ryan says.

San Diego's so expensive, especially compared to someplace like Maine. Zelia says that she and her mom will be able to buy a house there in a couple years, something they'd never be able to do here.

The air goes out of me as I realize something. Like, deep-down realize it.

Zelia's probably not going to come back here. Ever. For real.

It all hits me between the ribs. Zelia's being gone, and how she's cutting herself off from me. The house prices and Navegando Point. Suddenly all these battles feel like too much to deal with. They crush me as if they're real boulders on top of my shoulders.

"Who the heck is going to live here?" I stop moving so suddenly that Cecily bumps me. "What are all the non-rich people supposed to do in this town? Why do only the rich people get to enjoy the ocean?"

"What are you talking about?" Ryan swings around to look at me. "This neighborhood's nowhere near the ocean."

"Navegando Point is what I'm talking about."

Ryan crumples the flyer and sticks it in his pocket. "I have never needed ice cream more in my life." He takes off at a slow jog for the last half block, the rest of us following.

I think about the letter Nana Linda made me write. I don't know if all of us writing letters would be enough. But maybe this group could come up with some way that would really get people's attention. Or maybe Nana Linda has a new idea.

My grandfather's chilling on a lawn chair in the front yard, a glass of ice water in his hand. "Hey, Ava. Good to see you." He looks at my friends with mild curiosity in his deep brown eyes, as if I'm carrying a few extra books with me. "These are your reinforcements?" He takes a big, loud slurp.

Chad goes uncharacteristically quiet, looking down at his shoes.

Is he actually kind of shy with new people, or maybe

new adults? Dad has always forced me to say hello even if it was the last thing I wanted to do. Even if all I could manage was a whispered *hi*. Maybe Chad's insides feel like mine do when I have to do this, too.

I introduce them all, and they say hello.

"Good to meet you." Jīchan shakes each of their hands in a formal way.

"Your grass is the most evenly cut grass I've ever seen in my life." Ryan gets on his hands and knees to peer at it. "Is it fake?"

"Of course not," Jīchan says, squatting near Ryan and pulling out a blade. He chews it. "It's real."

"It's his baby," I say. "He cuts it with manicure scissors."

Ryan lets out a delighted gasp-giggle. "No way!"

Cecily and Chad bend to look at it, too. "Amazing!" Cecily says.

I'd always been afraid if I brought new people over, they'd think my grandparents were embarrassingly weird. But these kids think weird people are more interesting. I smile. I have a feeling that someone cutting grass with manicure scissors will end up in an improv scene soon.

Jīchan's a character. He does a lot of unique things. So is Nana Linda, for that matter. I tilt my head, considering my grandfather in a new light. Mom says I pay so much attention to detail because I'm a writer—maybe that will help me in improv as well.

Jīchan gets back up to a standing position—for an old man he can get up and down pretty well. He says sitting on the floor helps with mobility. "I admire people who can do improv. It looks so hard."

Everyone says that.

Ryan launches into a really detailed example of how the games work, and Jīchan's eyes start glazing over like mine do when Luke describes soccer plays.

"Let's do Improv 101 another time," I tell him. I open the screen door and we shuffle inside the house. "Take off your shoes." They kick off their shoes without question, leaving them in the neat rows next to my grandparents' sensible loafers and Mary Jane sneakers.

"Hello?" I call into the house.

"Nana will be home in a few minutes." Jīchan startles me by coming in behind us. "Now eat some ice cream. It's been on sale and we've been stockpiling." He hits his gut. "I can only take care of so much." He gestures at the kitchen. "Help yourselves."

"Oh boy!" Totally not caring that he's in a stranger's house, Chad runs toward the treats. A second later we hear the freezer door open. "It's like Baskin-Robbins in here!" he bellows. "Come check this out!"

"I'd better get them some bowls." Jīchan heads in there, Cecily following.

* * *

We're eating our ice cream around the dining table, when Nana Linda comes in, looking us over as if we're a bunch of nice gifts someone's left for her. "So great to meet all of you!"

I remember to introduce everyone. Each kid stands up and shakes her hand. "What nice manners!" She sits down next to Jīchan, who's scraping his spoon against the bowl.

They all look at me expectantly, as if I'm the one in charge. It's time to bring up our cause. I imagine my heart will start beating faster or something like I'm nervous, but nothing happens. Maybe my friends make me braver. Or the ice cream does. "Nana Linda, what else do you think we can do about Navegando Point?"

"Yeah, Ava told us what happened in the meeting." Ryan speaks around a mouthful of mint chip. "They should have let you talk."

"Well." Nana Linda leans back in her seat. "Does that mean you all are interested in helping our cause with more than an email? Because I have some ideas."

We all look at each other. I expect someone to say, *Why bother?* But everyone nods.

Nana Linda takes out her little laptop from her big bag. "Let's start with some research. Who wants to type?"

Cecily reaches for it. "I will."

"What about one of the historical landmarks?" Ryan

asks. "I saw a house with that. It had a plaque and everything."

"Google to the rescue." Cecily's fingers fly. "It's got to be fifty years old for the national landmark, and we've got fifteen more years for Navegando Point."

Jīchan speaks around a mouthful of butter pecan. "Check for local historic landmarks. San Diego only. I've seen those."

Cecily searches. "There is one." We gather around and read the description.

"I don't see anything about age limits," I say.

"Me neither."

"Maybe we're just not seeing it." Cecily does a search on the page. Nothing.

"No phone number for them," Nana Linda says. "Interesting. Let's send them an email."

"We need George Washington to have slept there or something," Chad says. "Or at least Richard Nixon."

"I kind of doubt anyone would care about Nixon," Ryan says.

"Look up the Facebook page," I say to Cecily.

"People still use Facebook?" Cecily squints.

"Old people do," Ryan says.

Nana Linda cough-laughs. "It's still a good way for groups to organize."

The Rescue Navegando Point Now! page has eleven thousand likes. That's a lot of people. There's a plan they came up with that's a compromise. I point it out. "Why don't the developers do this—just use the areas around Navegando Point but leave the old buildings alone?"

"Probably because it doesn't match their vision." Nana Linda peers at the screen. "It makes sense to me."

People aren't sharing the posts from the page, though, and there are only about a hundred likes on the news articles. I shake my head in frustration. "Do people just not care?"

"People tend to be apathetic unless something directly affects them," Nana Linda says.

We look at her blankly.

"Apathetic means they don't care. They're not moved to action," she explains. "So you might not care about Navegando Point closing unless you're personally affected."

"Like we are," Ryan says.

We're quiet for a minute. "But it actually affects a lot more people than just us." I tell Nana Linda about my thought on the way here. About how we won't be able to afford to buy a house or even go enjoy the water.

"Exactly right, munchkin." Nana Linda nods. "There's a ripple effect. Navegando Point businesses closing mean all those owners might lose their housing. The new businesses price out other, more affordable stores. Soon only the most well-off can enjoy living here."

"So . . ." Cecily puts her palms on the dining table.

"Let's start posting on social media and sharing with all those people. Tell them why they should take action."

"Oooh, let's write a blog post," Ryan says. "And share it to that page."

Nana Linda squints. "Yes, and let's also make a petition page with the link. Sound good? We'll send it to your parents to share with all their contacts."

"My mom has four thousand friends," Ryan says. "But only five she sees in real life."

"That's the way of social media," Nana Linda says drily.

And so we spend the next hour writing a blog post. The others help, brainstorming what to say. Well, Chad helps somewhat less, but it's all good.

The crushing-boulder feeling I had on the way here goes away.

For the first time since Brett Rosselin walked into our class, I get the sense that what we do might actually make some kind of difference.

CHAPTER 21

The second to last Monday of September, we have Cotillion. It maybe wouldn't be so bad if Dad didn't have to go early and leave late. But he does, so I'm here almost an extra two hours. "I want you to help this time," he tells me as he unlocks the auditorium doors. "Set up the chairs. Ask an adult what else you can do. Same as at home. Got it?"

I nod mutely.

The setup part goes quickly. To my surprise, I find that I actually feel better when I'm doing something instead of sitting doing nothing. I accidentally walk into a metal chair with my shins. Ouch. That'll bruise. I take blood thinners, which makes you bruise easily, so I've always got marks on me.

Today I'm wearing a dress, courtesy of Cecily, who'd found it at a thrift store at some point. It's long and black velvet, with sleeves that come down to my palms. Luke said I look like Morticia Addams in it, which I had to google. She's a witch character. I wanted to wear black lipstick, but Dad said absolutely not.

I sit in the middle of the other girls. It's too bad Cecily's not taking Cotillion; it'd be nice to have a friend here. Everyone else is in their groups. It's not at all like improv. I look around. I actually recognize a lot of them from my classes, either new to me this year or from elementary school. I bet they don't even know my name.

Kiley, Becca, and Cherine sit near me again. Tonight they're talking about Mr. Sukow's commercial project. Also known as the Longest Project in the History of America. They must have him during a different period.

"Who can make a napkin interesting?" Becca rolls her eyes.

"Yeah. I wanted the margarine container, but I got an extension cord," Kiley says.

I clear my throat. "I have the napkin, too." They don't hear me because they're all louder and faster talkers than I am. My voice is as lost as a whisper during a heavy-metal concert.

I slump down. I wish Dad could see this conversation happening. Then maybe he'd understand where I was coming from when I said how hard it is to talk to people.

If Dad were here instead of me, he'd just talk and they'd listen. It's like I'm always wearing an invisibility cloak that makes people stop listening. I'm not competitive like my brothers or my mom; I have a hard time telling people what to do.

Then I remember Ryan. As long as he's conscious, he has a hard time shutting up. But he listens to me. Sometimes I think he has to make a big effort to do it, but he does do it.

I mean, everyone's capable of toning it down, right? If I can turn it up, they can turn it down. "I'm in Mr. Sukow's fifth period," I say, making my voice a little louder, as if I'm in improv class. The girls turn to look at me, ready to hear what I've got to say. "I have the napkin, too," I repeat, louder, squeezing my hands nervously against the material of my dress. The velvet feels nice and soft, and I want to pet it like it's a kitten but that might also look weird, to have me petting my leg like a small animal. "I have an idea for what might help."

There's a small silence. "Sure," the black-haired girl, Cherine, says. "I'm totally stuck."

I tell her about the improv game, how you can think about what napkin reminds you of and brainstorm from there.

"You do improv? Like on that TV show?" Kiley says, as if I've said, *I can fly like Superman.* "But you're so quiet! I didn't even think you could talk!"

"Kiley!" Cherine says. "Rude much?"

My cheeks burn. Does *everybody* have to have this reaction?

"I could never do improv," Cherine says. "Just get on

stage and make stuff up?" She shudders dramatically, making the blue sequins on her top jingle-jangle. "No thank you. How scary."

"Yeah, I don't even want to do this commercial project, and we get to *practice* it." Becca pulls her creamy cardigan around her. "That you do improv is totally incredible."

They all look at me admiringly. I stare at the floor. "Thanks." Okay, so I talked and they talked back. What now? I swallow and give them a tiny smile, so they know I'm not being snooty. They smile back.

What else can I say? I think about improv again, and that makes me think of Navegando Point, and the meeting Nana Linda and I went to last week. "Um, did you know that Navegando Point is getting torn down?"

"Which one is that?" Cherine says.

"The one with the haunted house?" Becca says.

"No. That's Old Town. Navegando Point is by the water. With the old shops," Kiley informs them. She leans over to me and I notice her brown eyes are lined with royal blue, making them pop. "And the carousel."

"Oh, I like that place, but my parents say it's too touristy." Cherine cocks her head to the side. "They're tearing it down?"

"Yeah," Becca says. "My mom wanted to go to her favorite Greek place the other day and it's totally dark."

"That's my dad's favorite restaurant, too." Maybe they

can write letters. But those would probably be ignored, as well.

Sometimes I wish I weren't eleven years old. If I were a fifty-year-old lawyer, I could probably figure out what to do.

Then Dad comes out in the middle of the room, telling us about the dance we're going to do, and I'm sorry for more than one reason. Partly because I have to dance now. But mostly because I finally was able to say what I wanted to some people and it—surprise—did not end with me going down in flames, and I wonder why I've never done it before. I wish I had.

Whatever you say is the right thing to say. Another improv motto.

Becca and I exchange a smile as we stand up, waiting for the dance.

I'm paired with a kid who's surprisingly tall for a sixth grader. He's wearing an actual suit instead of the dress shirt and slacks most of the other boys are wearing, navy blue with a bright red tie. "I'm Armando," he says. His voice hasn't changed yet even though he's taller than I am.

I click down the list of what Dad tells us to do. Introduce yourself. Start dancing. "I'm Ava." It occurs to me that Cotillion is sort of like improv—we have to remember to do a bunch of stuff, and if we do it enough, it's supposed to become natural. Or something.

Armando gives me a quick nod. His hands are sweating like crazy, and I sort of pull down on my sleeves so his hands aren't directly against mine, then wonder if that's against the rules.

Normally I'd be annoyed and counting the seconds until the dance was over, but today I feel . . . I don't know. Worried about him. Wanting to make him comfortable. I show Armando the steps again. "It's actually easier if you don't look down. I know the steps, so you could just kind of follow me."

His scuffed black shoes slowly shuffle along in rhythm with me. "I think I got it. Is this good?"

"Good enough." I hold out my hand. He takes it and I rest my other hand on his shoulder. Now that he's looking at me instead of the floor, we're not nearly as clumsy.

"What's your favorite subject at school?" I ask him.

"Math." He ducks his head shyly. "We're doing integers."

Now I don't have to pretend to find something in common. It's funny because normally I might pretend to be interested, even though I'm not. Because I'm looking for ways to be genuinely interested in what he's saying, I *am*. "Oh, really? We're doing those, too."

He starts telling me about some mathematician from the 1700s and his influence on math, and instead of tuning him out like I normally would, I really listen and pick out the stuff I relate to. I tell him about my mom's job and how good she is at math.

"That's nice," the boy says, then goes back to talking about math history.

He's ignoring Dad's rules. I know this boy likes rules because he likes math, therefore he should be able to follow them if he tries. Maybe if I point them out. "Excuse me," I say when he takes a breath. "Da—I mean, Mr. Andrews's rules state that you should ask a question in return when someone offers information." I squinch up my shoulders. "I did it. You should, too."

The boy blinks as he processes this. "You're right," he says at last. "I haven't been following the rules very well. I'm sorry. I'm nervous about the dancing." He blushes. "What kind of engineer is your mom? I want to be an engineer."

Finally.

I guess nobody goes to Cotillion because they're already perfect.

The second dance goes about the same, except this kid knows the steps better. I even relax enough to laugh.

I glance at Dad, who gives me a thumbs-up. This is all for Zelia, I remind myself. So I can visit. I remember our last call with a little pang.

If she still wants me to, that is.

After class, Dad's talking to a lady who's got her arm around Becca. He catches my eye and motions me over. I go to him, but try to stand as far away as possible without being totally rude. He knows I'm uncomfortable with strangers.

"Ava, this is Mrs. Ladigan, Becca's mom. She took Cotillion from your grandfather." Dad looks smug, like he always does when people compliment him on Cotillion or tell him that his dad did a great job.

"Cotillion is a brilliant experience for a child." Mrs. Ladigan beams. With her perfectly blown-out brown hair, she reminds me of a TV reporter. "It taught me so much confidence. Of course, I hated it at the time." She and Dad laugh.

Wow. That's the first time I've heard an adult admit it. I hold out my hand almost automatically, the way I've been trained. *Don't mumble*, I remind myself, and don't. "Hi. Nice to meet you."

She shakes it. "Your father tells me you're working on a plan to save Navegando Point."

I turn bright red. Or I think I do, since I can't actually see myself. I should say, *Yes, I am. Would you like to write letters?* But my throat won't work.

Luckily, Mrs. Ladigan doesn't seem to expect a response. Because she went to Cotillion, she's all about not embarrassing me. "I'm an environmental attorney. I deal with land-use stuff a lot. Maybe I can suggest some things."

I nod mutely.

"That would be great!" Dad says. "Thank you so much."

"No problem." She digs into her purse and produces a business card, passing it to me. "Email me."

I nod again, relieved. Email I can do. Phone calls are another thing.

She and Becca leave, and Dad turns to me. "That sounds promising, and it was very generous of her. Are you going to take her up on it?"

"Did she mean it?" I turn the card over in my hands. The letters stick up and it looks super fancy. My first business card. The thought of emailing her makes me sweaty and it only happened about three seconds ago.

"Of course she meant it. I didn't ask her. She could have just said good night and left."

"But Mom's always telling people we run into that they should have lunch, and she never does." Promising extra stuff just seems like a grown-up thing to do.

Dad bends and looks in my eyes. "All you can do is reach out. The rest is up to her."

I nod. Reaching out seems like it should be easy enough. "It's just an email, right?"

"That's right." He claps a hand on my shoulder. "Now let's get you home."

CHAPTER 22

Miss Gwen ends up renting a classroom at the Mission Valley Library. This is one of my favorite libraries, not only because it's newer, with a second story, but also because it's right next to an IKEA. Which means every time I go, I ask my parents if we can get meatballs. They say yes only once in a while, but it's still worth an ask.

"Don't talk to strangers," Dad calls after me as I shut the car door. "Go to the front desk if you have a problem."

"Dad! I know. I'm in sixth grade." I turn away. A couple of older teenage girls walk by and smile at me, probably thinking my dad's too overprotective. I pretend like I don't know who he is and get myself inside.

I walk into the main room past the check-out desk. The first person I see is Miss Gwen, sitting at one of the long tables in the middle of the room with her laptop in front of her. "Ah, just who I was hoping to see! How are you, Ava?" She pats the seat beside her.

I sit, my bottom making a little squeaking noise on the vinyl seat cushion. "I'm fine. I'm sorry the theater closed." I want to ask her why she told us not to worry, but what good will it do at this point?

"Your grandmother emailed me." Miss Gwen looks at me with seriousness. "She told me about the Port of San Diego meeting."

I squish my shoulders down. "We all wrote letters, but I don't know if they even read them."

She sighs. "Probably not. They decided what was happening well before the public hearing. The developers give a lot of money to politicians."

That sounds like what Nana Linda was saying. The thought of them doing whatever they want makes me mad. "Then why do they even bother with a public hearing?"

"To make it seem legit."

"But . . . that's not right." My face heats up like it's been doing lately when I hear about injustice. I never cared about stuff like this before. Now it's like I'm a superhero who's always on the lookout for crime. Ava the Activist. All I need is a cape.

"A lot of things aren't right, Ava." Miss Gwen gives me a small, regretful smile, then glances at her watch. "It's about time for class. I don't want you to worry about it, okay? We'll find a new spot for the theater. It'll just take time." She logs off the computer and stands.

"Do you know where?"

She shakes her head. "No. There aren't too many theater spaces. Maybe we can rent an empty storefront and build one." Miss Gwen begins walking to the other side of the library, where the classrooms are. "But we'll have to get a new loan for that, and new permits—lots of things to think about."

I tell Miss Gwen about the blog post. Our parents have shared it, but nothing much has happened. Only about ten people have signed the petition so far.

"We really appreciate it, Ava." Miss Gwen pats my arm and looks kind of sad.

Ryan arrives after Miss Gwen turns on the classroom lights. "Hey." He sets his backpack on a chair and sits down, leaving three spaces between us.

"Hey," I manage.

"I'm going to run out and flag down everyone," Miss Gwen says. "Don't go anywhere." She leaves.

Ryan and I sit and stare at the white wall. I wonder what he's thinking about. How much he dislikes me? Flamin' Hot Cheetos? It could be anything.

Suddenly it strikes me that I'll never know the answer to what's going on in Ryan's head—or anyone's head. If I did, I would make a bazillion dollars as a mind reader. The realization makes my tense muscles relax.

I actually think of a good question to ask him, something Ryan would know. "Did you have Mr. Sukow for English last year?"

"I did." He looks sideways at me. "Are you doing the 'make a boring object interesting' project?"

"Yeah." I shake my head. "I am *not* getting along with my partner. He totally hates me."

"Well. You know what? Not everyone's going to like you." Ryan shrugs. "I mean, when we perform, not everybody laughs at the same thing. It doesn't mean it's not funny. Who cares if this person doesn't like you?"

Ryan must be from Mars. Who doesn't care about being liked? "It makes it hard to do the assignment." I tilt my head at him. "Do you like everyone in the group?"

"Sure. But I'm not besties with everyone." Ryan scratches his head. "Like, Jonathan's always doing stuff that I think is kind of weird. But that's my problem. Plus, it's always stuff I would never think of in a billion years. And that's pretty cool." Ryan flashes me a grin. He's got a dimple, and two light-colored moles on his cheek. I don't know why I'm noticing that.

It makes me wonder what he notices about me.

It also makes me remember that I've got a scabbed-over zit on the side of my nose. Suddenly I'm all self-conscious again. I move away. "Um, well, what if that person is also kind of mean to you?"

"Like a bully?"

I shrug. "Not exactly."

"He's probably got something going on," Ryan says quietly. "Something that's not good. That's what happened when my parents were getting a divorce. I wasn't so nice to others." He crosses his arms. "Maybe he just needs a friend."

I wrinkle my nose. It's hard to be Ty's friend when I'm always frozen up around him. I sigh out my entire insides, then change the subject. "So what's your favorite subject?" I remember to ask. Dad would be proud.

"Lunch." Ryan laughs.

At the end of class, Miss Gwen has us get into our closing circle to say goodbye. "Remember," she says. "Follow the fun. Always follow the fun."

"Which is also my life motto," says Ryan.

I smile. I like that motto a lot. In fact, I'm liking improv a lot. Every time I go, I feel better about it. Like it's not just a way for me to prove something, but it's actually fun. Kind of like when Zelia and I played pretend—except now, there's not just one person leading the whole thing. We're making stories together.

"I want to say, also, that I'm not sure about the future of the theater, but we will definitely be able to finish our classes." She gives us a quick smile. "So don't worry."

"Too late," Cecily says.

"However . . ." Miss Gwen's smile fades. "I don't know about next semester."

My heart drops.

"Yeah, the Port of San Diego didn't even respond to the email I sent last week," Ryan says.

"Mine either," Chad says.

"Or mine," Cecily says.

"What else can we do? We set up the petition with Nana Linda." Cecily shakes her head.

I think about Becca's mom. My palms sweat. It's been four days and I still haven't emailed her.

My heart thumps. I clear my throat, getting ready to speak up. The rest of them go quiet and turn and look at me. It's like they're getting used to me—getting used to letting me have the space I need to say something. "Hey. Um. I think there's probably more stuff we can do." I start sweating. "My dad knows this lady." I tell them about Mrs. Ladigan.

"Yes!" Cecily says. "You email her and we'll meet— how about Wednesday after school? It's a short day."

"We can meet at the library this time," Ryan says.

"As for me, I'm currently doing as much as I want to," Jonathan says. He gives us a nod. "But let me know if you want more letters." He leaves without waiting for another word from anyone.

"Does he not like us?" I ask Cecily in a low voice.

"He's just really introverted. He told me once that improv was all the social time he could handle. That's cool." Cecily shrugs. "Everyone's different."

I'm introverted, too, but also have social anxiety,

which I suppose means I'm shy. I wish I weren't shy, that I could spend more time with people. Jonathan's happy alone. That's different than how I feel.

Babel shakes her head. "This is going to be all I can do, too. But you guys should meet if you want."

I nod. I'm going to email Mrs. Ladigan if it's the last thing I do. "I'm in."

CHAPTER 23

That evening, Zelia FaceTimes me to tell me about her giving Willy Wonka a bath. It's a funny story, but my mind's on improv and Navegando Point. "He fell all the way in! He was so mad at me." Zelia giggles.

"Poor Willy Wonka."

"I know." She strokes his fur. "I injured his pride."

"So." I kind of cough up this word, working up to telling Zelia. Because last time she was sort of weird about me talking about improv and I want to make sure she doesn't get that way again. "The improv kids and I are trying to save Navegando Point. Because cupcakes."

"Huh," she says.

I tell her what we've done so far, and what we might do. "And who knows? Nana Linda just might chain herself to a building. You know how she is." I chuckle.

She wrinkles her nose. "Oh my gosh, Ava. Do you have any idea how much you talk about improv?"

I shake my head. "Not that much." Because she won't let me.

"I never talked about it that much with you," she says sharply. "'Cause it's not that interesting. And neither is Navegando Point. It's all broke-down like a bunch of shacks anyway."

"I talk about it because they're my friends." A little shiver comes over me when I say this. "And Navegando Point isn't a bunch of shacks. It's charming." That's what my parents call it.

She rolls her eyes. "It's falling apart."

"Zelia!" Zelia's mom comes in, looking a little annoyed. "Why aren't you asleep? Lights-out time!" She peers at the phone. "Oh, hi, sweet Ava. I guess you can stay up ten more minutes," she says to Zelia.

Her mom walking in makes the tension between us zap away, mostly. Maybe that's Zelia's problem—she's tired. Now my heart melts a tiny bit. I haven't seen Zelia's mom since they moved. She looks exactly like an older version of her daughter. A sort of stretched-taller Zelia. "Hi, Gaby."

"I miss you." She waves at me.

"I miss you, too. Do you like your new job?"

"I love it!" Gaby puts her arm around Zelia. "It's an adjustment, but we're getting there, right, Zelia?"

"Right." Zelia moves away from her.

Her mom blows a kiss at me, and I pretend to catch

it. "See you later, love," she says. "Work hard. Do your best." That's Zelia's mom's motto.

"I will," I say. She leaves the room and I wait for Zelia to tell me what's really going on, why she rolled her eyes. But she doesn't say anything for a minute, just braids the hair by her face in that nervous way she has when she's thinking about something. I remember Ryan saying that sometimes when people act out, there's something else going on. "Is everything okay?" I ask finally.

"Yeah."

"You like it there, don't you?" I squint at her.

"It's fine."

Suddenly I'm very tired. Like I want to go to sleep just so I don't have to talk to her anymore. "Zelia . . ." I begin, not sure what I'm going to say.

"Hey. I've got to go to bed," Zelia says. I can tell she's still annoyed with me.

"Okay." I think it would hurt less if she slapped me across my face.

"Okay."

We stare at each other for a second. It wasn't just the Jelly Bellies. As I've been realizing over the last couple months, I've always been Zelia's follower. If there are two ways that something could be done, we usually did it Zelia's way. For example, when we were drawing a graphic novel this last summer, I wanted to use a Sailor Moon style, like anime, and she wanted to do it in a more realistic style. Guess which way we did it? If there are two cookies left and one's chocolate chocolate chip, which we both love, and one's oatmeal raisin, which we both are meh about, I let her have the chocolate chocolate chip. But if I somehow got that one, I'd break it in half and let her choose which piece she wanted.

She should think more about me first. Or at least equally.

I take a breath and feel my heart hammering in my chest. I swallow. "Good night."

"Good night," she says.

After we hang up, I stare at the ceiling for a while. How can two people be talking about the same thing but seem to be talking about two entirely different things?

I might as well do something productive. Slowly, I type out an email to Mrs. Ladigan. *Thank you for your very generous offer of assistance. We could use all the suggestions we can get.* I list what we've done. For a second, I want to delete it. What if she thinks we're stupid?

No, Ava. Just do it.

This time it's not Zelia's voice in my head. Just mine.

A little roar erupts out. I'm going to own being a superhero. "Yes!" I fist-bump the air. "Ava Andrews, Activist, at your service." Then I hit send. Who cares that I close my eyes when I do it? Nobody can see but me.

CHAPTER 24

On Wednesday after school, I shoot out of class and head over to the library to meet the others. Chad and Cecily are already there. We planned to go use the conference room inside.

She waves. "Hey! Bad news. The library's closed after school."

"What do you mean, closed?" Ryan tries the lock as if his touch can open it, as if he's Arthur pulling the magic sword out of the stone. Of course nothing happens.

"I guess I've never tried coming on a Wednesday." I'm the library helper. Why don't I know all the hours? I look away from my friends. "I'm sorry. I should have checked." Now we don't have a place to practice, and it's all because of me.

"Don't be sorry," Cecily says. "It's not your fault. Any of us could have looked at the hours."

I swallow and meet her eyes, green behind her glasses.

She doesn't look mad at all. She's moved on.

Good idea. "Well, we could see if Mr. Sukow will let us use his classroom."

Then Chad brightens. "I know what we can do. Go to Fosters Freeze!"

Cecily bumps me with her arm. "How about you? You up for the Freeze?"

My heart seems to skip. This is my chance! "Sure." Now that I've spent time with Cecily, I'm confident that she really does want to hang out with me.

Chad points his index finger at the rest of us. "You guys in?" He puts his backpack on. "My stomach's eating itself."

"I don't have any money," Cecily says.

"I'll give you some," Ryan and I say at the same time.

"Heck, if you two are giving out money, I could use an extra shake." Chad starts running. "Let's go already."

We follow him down the sidewalk. And so, before I know quite what's happening, I'm fulfilling my and Zelia's old dream. Even though I hear her voice in my head telling me it's gross, it's not. I like it even if she doesn't.

That might be like the most disloyal thought I've ever had about Zelia.

Fosters Freeze has two parts. There's a restaurant din-ing area, and a walk-up outdoor counter. It looks like it was built in the 1950s and it probably was. They sell hamburgers and fries but also lots of soft-serve ice-cream things—shakes and cones—and the regular ice cream.

Ryan walks up to the counter. Saunters is more like it. A teenage girl probably about sixteen is working, wearing a paper hat and a white uniform. "Ready to order?" she says to him.

"I reckon so." Ryan's got a Texas accent for some reason. "Yep, yep, yep."

I guess Ryan thought this would entertain the girl, but her nose wrinkles and she kind of sighs. "So are you going to tell me what you want or not?"

Ryan wilts, all his normal energy draining out of him. "A small dipped vanilla cone, please."

I feel bad for him. "I reckon I'd like the same," I say in my own Texas accent.

"Make that three, pardner," Cecily adds.

"Four, y'all. Yee-haw," Chad says.

This makes all four of us giggle. We slide our money onto the counter at the same time.

"Weirdos." She sighs, turns away, and starts piling the cake cones with soft serve, then dipping them into a vat of chocolate sauce. When she lifts out the cones, the chocolate hardens instantly. She hands them to us one after another.

I wonder how Zelia would feel if she could see me. If

she were here, would she really refuse to come? I kind of doubt it.

A thought hits me with a sharp tang, like a bite of lemon. Maybe Zelia only liked me when I didn't have anything of my own going on. When I sat around waiting for her to help me and she could be my boss.

Could that be true? If Zelia were here, she would definitely take the lead and I'd be as quiet as ever, wishing I could speak up.

Or would we both be happy, sitting here with everyone?

We move over to the concrete table on the little patio. I take a bite of chocolate-covered ice cream. The soft serve's already leaking through, and I'm going to have to eat fast before it drips down my arm. My phone pings. It's Mrs. Ladigan. "Guys, she responded!" I say.

Ryan bites into his cone, leaving a creamy goatee-shaped stain under his mouth. "Well, tell us what she said already."

I read Mrs. Ladigan's message. "She says we should go talk to the public and get some grassroots support. In person. Like hand out flyers at Navegando Point, or go knock on doors." My stomach jumps. Talk to strangers? No thanks. I read the rest aloud. *"You have eleven thousand people who theoretically care. But the way to really get them to care is by putting a face to the problem."*

"Well." Cecily wipes her mouth. "We *are* super-cute kids." She flutters her eyelashes.

"I vote for trying flyers first." Somehow Ryan's already halfway done with his cone.

I nod, trying to eat mine before it totally melts. That sounds better than knocking on doors. I just have to hand them flyers. I can do that.

"Settled!" Chad is actually finished eating. He wipes his hands with a napkin, runs out of napkin, and uses his shorts to get the rest of the soft serve off. "Anyone want to do some improv?"

Ryan gets up. "Sure. Might as well, since we're together."

My face goes hot. Again. "Here? We can't do improv here."

"You can do improv anywhere." Ryan gestures at me to stand.

So I do. My knees are shaking a little bit. What if people stare? "Zap." I point at Cecily. I forget that we're in public, though, because I'm half-focused on not letting my cone drip and half-focused on the game.

That's how we end up doing Zip-Zap-Zop outside Fosters Freeze. People stop and watch. A man smoking a cigarette in the parking lot seems especially concerned. "What is that?" he says in a loud voice to the man next to him. "Some kind of cult?"

"Probably. There's a church in that storefront over there." The other man blows smoke into the air. I cough as it drifts over.

I guess maybe we do look like some kind of cult or something, chanting like we are. Still, it's funny that people think we're a religion. "Those men think we're a cult," I inform my teammates. "The Fosters Freeze Cult."

Ryan hoots.

"That has got to be our improv team name!" Cecily says. "If Babel and Jonathan agree."

"Woot!" Chad says.

I smile, concentrating on my friends and my friends alone. Pretty soon I forget anyone else is around. Nobody's really paying attention to us anyway.

"What do you want to do?" Cecily asks.

"How about One Word?" I say. That's where you tell a story going around in a circle, and each person says just a single word or punctuation mark. It's easy but also difficult because you start getting an idea of how you want the story to go but you have to listen to what the other people say.

And that means you have to change your expectations. Go with what you're actually hearing instead of what you expect.

That's really, really hard for me. I think I'm getting better, though, and the stories we make up are terrible and silly. By the time we finish that game, our cones are gone.

Cecily calls to the smoking man in the parking lot. "Sir! Can you give me a suggestion for a place that doesn't exist in reality?"

"Huh?" He coughs. "Oz!"

Oz makes me think of red shoes, which makes me think of Luke's cleats. I step into the small concrete square between the tables and pretend I'm throwing stuff out of a closet. Cecily comes out. "Mom, you put my cleats in the wrong place!" I tell her.

"I'm not your maid." Cecily pretends to bang down a basket of laundry. "Put these clothes away, mister."

Uh-oh. I don't know where to take this. I don't want to have a scene about silly soccer cleats and laundry. Who cares about that? What's the scene really about? My character's upset about something. But what?

Just then, a familiar old Toyota Camry pulls up. I almost jump out of my skin. I know that car—it's Hudson. With Luke.

Both of them give me the kind of death glare Mom gives Luke when he farts in public. They practically leap out of the car.

"Ava!" Hudson reaches us first. "You need to tell someone if you're going somewhere."

"Yeah," Luke says. "This parking lot is sketchy. There's a bar right there!"

"Shush." Chad motions Hudson to the bench. "We're improvising."

"Improv," Luke kind of sneers, "is not an excuse."

I put my hands on my hips. "You're not the boss of me."

Chad snaps his fingers as if he's applauding. "She told you."

"I'm older, so that automatically makes me the boss." Luke scowls.

"You don't act older," I mutter.

"All right, you two." Hudson grabs Luke's hand and hauls him down to the bench. "We can watch."

Cecily turns back to me. "It's very upsetting that you won't do your chores," Cecily says to me, but we've lost our rhythm with the interruption.

Then I get an idea. Time to use what Miss Gwen calls The Reveal.

"The truth is," I say to her, "there's this bully at school."

Cecily twists her face into an O of surprise. "Oh my. What's he doing to you?"

I think of Luke and Ty. But what if it were the opposite of bad? What if it were something I actually wanted? *Reverse expectations* is another thing Miss Gwen tells us. "He's always like, 'Hey, can I carry those books for you? Hey, you're so smart. You're so kind.' I'm sick of it."

Everyone laughs. Even Luke cracks a smile.

There's a good energy in the air now, and Cecily goes with it. This is the game, the fun part. "I don't blame you. I'd be sick of it, too. All those terrible comments. Why, I have a mind to call the principal right now!" Cecily makes the call.

Ryan steps in, answering. "This is the principal."

"This is Conrad's mother."

"Oh, just the person I wanted to speak with. I have bad news for you. Conrad's getting an award."

"Noooo," Cecily groans.

There's a big laugh now. Chad runs across stage in front of us to show the scene's over. Miss Gwen says it's best to end on the biggest laugh.

I high-five Cecily. "Awesome job," I whisper to her.

Hudson and Luke are looking at me as if I've traveled back in time and stopped the Civil War. Hudson's mouth is open. "What. Was. That."

I look sideways at Luke. Will he know the scene was about him? I didn't mean for it to be—it just came out. "Improv."

My brothers are silent. I don't know if it's a good silent or a bad silent.

Luke clears his throat. "I've never seen you talk that much in public. Why can't you be like that all the time?"

I squish my shoulders up to my ears, heat surging through me. Luke always has to call me out. I don't know why I can't be like this wherever I go. If I could, life would be a lot simpler.

Ryan speaks up. "It's different."

"It shouldn't be." Luke crosses his arms and squints at me as if I've been pulling a fast one on my family with my anxiety for the past eleven years.

If he tells me to get it together, I am going to scream. I open my mouth to say—I don't know what—but Hudson steps in, pulling cash out of his pocket. "Might as well get a cone while we're here," he says to Luke, and Luke turns to the window. Hudson winks at me.

I sag into relief. At least one of my brothers has my back. I'll have to be okay with that for now. "Might as well."

CHAPTER 25

That evening, I should be working on my napkin project, but I've pretty much given up on that for now. And by *given up*, I mean it's like the time I had to do a science project and kept putting it off until the night before. I didn't even give my parents the sheet about it. They let me get a minus mark on that—that's the elementary school version of failing.

I'll probably fail this napkin project, too. But does it matter? What's the worst thing that could happen? My parents aren't going to disown me or kick me out. If Ty isn't going to try, I decide, then I'm not, either.

Instead, I'm designing a flyer for Navegando Point on my laptop and watching *Jeopardy!* with my parents. Nobody ever beats Mom—I don't know why she hasn't been a contestant.

I show a draft to my parents. "What do you think?" I put a photo of the carousel and ice cream on the flyer, plus the website where people can go. Dad says to get it done a week in advance, and he'll get them printed so we can hand them out.

"Looks good," Dad says. "But I'd do a different, unifying color for the background instead of plain white."

I shrug.

Mom wiggles her fingers. "Want me to give it a shot?"

"Go for it." I hand her the computer. Then my phone rings in my bedroom. It might be Cecily! I race so fast down the hallway my socks almost skid out from under me on the hardwood. "Wait!" I call, as if that's going to help. I reach the phone just in time by flinging myself across my bed and answer without looking at the caller ID. I land a little too far to the left and feel the pinch of my ICD pacemaker, as if I've fallen into the edge of a table. "Oooof," I say into Zelia's face. "Hi." I swallow hard. I haven't talked to her since last week, when we had our weird kind-of argument that her mom interrupted.

She takes a breath. "Hey, Ava." Then neither of us says anything. I might tell her about the flyers, but she doesn't want to hear about that. Or my improv. Or anything.

The silence goes on so long it gets downright weird. I sort of wish I hadn't answered.

I play with my hair. "So, what's up?"

Zelia speaks flatly, the way she does when she gives someone bad news. "I wanted to talk to you about coming out here."

I sit on my bed and put my pillow on my lap. "It's not even Halloween. Do I have to decide right now?"

Zelia twirls her hair around a finger. "Everyone here is already setting up their summer camps and stuff."

"Okay." I wait.

"So I don't think you should come. Because I'm probably going to do that." She doesn't look at the camera.

My heart seems to literally sink. "I'm only coming for two weeks—can't you go to camp the rest of the time?"

She lets go of her hair, and it bounces like a spring. "I'm just trying to make it easier for you. You won't have to do Cotillion."

Wait, what? Sure, I've complained about Cotillion before to Zelia because I was worried about doing it. But I haven't complained since I made the deal with my parents. "Cotillion's not that bad." I can't get my mind wrapped around this. She doesn't want me, at all? My eyes burn. I blink them quickly.

"It's not?"

I purse my lips, thinking about quitting Cotillion. That feels like I'd be getting out of the thing that both my brothers had to do. Like the time I got out of cleaning the bathroom. "It's really . . . sort of okay."

"Hmmm," she says.

My heart speeds up. Just like I promised Zelia I would with those Jelly Bellies, I'm going to tell her what I want. It's been building up and up. I have to do it now and find out if she actually likes me when I'm *not* doing what she wants. "I . . ." I swallow, then force it out. "I *want* to come visit you."

She blinks. "You do?"

Relief whooshes out of me, water draining from a sink. "Yeah. I really, really do." That's what I've been working on.

"Oh." Zelia's eyebrows pull together.

I chew on a hangnail. Now's the part where she's supposed to tell me she's glad I said something about what I really want. She's supposed to say, *Oh, I get it, you come out to Maine!* But she doesn't.

Instead we sort of don't look at each other.

She takes in a breath. "Well, I guess maybe I don't need you to."

Now it's like she's twisting a knife in my side. Tears start falling for real and I bite my tongue. I don't want her to see them. "You don't need me to?" I repeat quietly so she can't hear the shake in my voice.

She still won't meet my eyes. "I have my stuff in Maine. You have your stuff in California. It's going to be busy."

I swallow. I can think of two reasons for Zelia acting this way. One: she doesn't want me to visit because she doesn't like me anymore.

Two: Zelia really wasn't a good friend for me. Because good friends don't just ignore what their friends say.

I'm afraid of either reason. Zelia hates me. Now that

she's gone to Maine, she's realized it. I was too needy and she hates improv.

I don't think I can handle it if I find out that Zelia is deep-down mean inside. If that's true, then all of elementary school was a lie.

"Say something."

"What do you want me to say?" My voice is sharp and loud, hiding the hurt I'm feeling.

My chest burns, and it's not because I just ate something spicy. "I'm still not going to quit improv if that's what you want."

"Why would I want you to do that?"

"I don't know—you said it was stupid." My heart seems to skip. "I guess you're right—I'll be too busy with all my new friends, just like you are with yours." I want her to be as hurt as I am. Then I feel bad for wanting that. I touch my ICD pacemaker.

My phone buzzes with a text. Ty's number.

"Oh," I say, surprised. "It's my napkin project partner."

Zelia's eyebrows go up.

Can you meet after school on Monday so we can get this done with.

K, I reply.

"Well, I'm going to let you get back to that," Zelia says.

"Yeah," I say.

We pause for a second.

"Bye," Zelia says.

"Bye."

She closes her app first. I sigh. We didn't settle anything. In fact, things feel even worse now than they did before. Like an argument that turns in a circle, spinning around and around without an end. I turn off the light in my room and sit in the dark for a long time.

CHAPTER 26

Dad always uses a printing press for his Cotillion stuff, so he ordered me a bunch of flyers for our cause. On Saturday, after our improv class, our parents carpool us over to Navegando Point. Then we're going in groups of two along the path to hand them out. The parents will be there, too, but mostly supervising.

It's a sunny day, so there's a ton of people around. It's not as busy as it is during the summertime, when people are here on vacation, but the parking lot's almost full and there are a lot of families. Most locals go to places like this after the tourists have gone home—I know my family does.

Cecily pairs with her dad and Babel, Chad pairs with Jonathan and Jonathan's mom, and Ryan pairs with me and my dad. Then we go over by the carousel.

Ryan, of course, is way better at this than I am. "Do you really want to see this fine attraction close forever?"

he bellows. He even stands on a bench at one point. People can't help but look at him.

I hold out a flyer to a family waiting in line at the carousel. "Excuse me . . ."

They ignore me, walking past as the line moves up.

"Hey!" the ride operator calls to me. "Don't bother my customers."

My eyes go so wide that I can feel wind on the tops of my eyeballs. "Sorry, sorry." I back away into the crowd.

"Just go over here." Dad turns me around. "I don't think that's an actual rule, but we'll do as he asks."

I nod mutely, the operator's words ringing in my ears. I want to leave right now. Why did I ever think this was a good idea?

"Shake it off, Ava. It doesn't matter. Okay?"

I swallow. "Okay."

I thrust another flyer at a random person, not looking in their eyes like I'm supposed to. "Um, they're closing . . ."

"No thanks," the person responds.

We do this for another half hour. Then Ryan runs over to me. "I'm all out of flyers! How about you?"

I hold up my fat stack, wanting to hide. "I'm terrible at this."

"You're doing fine." Ryan claps a hand on my shoulder. "Want me to stand with you?"

Ryan and I manage to hand out the rest together. He

does the talking and I do the handing. Then we reconvene with the rest of the group by the closed ice-cream shop.

"Success!" Cecily pumps her fist in the air.

"Now let's see if we got any new likes." Babel whips out her phone.

We crane our necks over her shoulder to see. Nope.

"They haven't had time yet," Cecily's dad says.

The group sighs as one. The parents exchange glances, like they're wondering what to do with us. "Anyone want a cupcake?" Dad asks.

"I thought you'd never ask." I lead the way.

We walk past the duck pond and, as my feet hit the path near it, my stomach drops for the thousandth time that day.

Our flyers are all over the place. Scattered under benches. Crumpled and tossed to the side. A gull caws and swoops down and poops on one.

"Crud." Cecily runs to pick one up. "They couldn't even put them in the trash?"

Not only did we fail, we created actual litter. Great. That's not going to help anything. We spread out and collect them. When I go to throw mine away in the big trash can, I see even more stuffed in there.

"Did everyone just throw them out?" I shake my head. "What a waste."

"It's not . . . at least everyone saw them first." Dad

catches up to me. "You know, in marketing, it takes seven contacts before people take any action. That means they've got to see something seven different times. That was their first contact." But even he looks a little sad.

"Still, it's terrible that people just throw this stuff around," Jonathan's mom says.

We're all quiet for a minute, staring at the trash. But the cupcake shop will raise our spirits.

When we round the corner to the shop, though, the whole corridor is completely dark. Chad runs ahead. "Closed," he reports.

I peer into the window at the empty cases. Where did the workers go? What will the owner do? Where will I ever get cupcakes that good again? I turn, and my friends look just as disappointed as I do. There's nothing else left to say. Without agreeing to it, we all walk out to the parking lot and go on home.

CHAPTER 27

After school on Monday, I'm supposed to meet Ty at the public library. It's packed. Toddlers run at full speed through the aisles, tired moms and dads chasing after. Adults use the computers and take up the tables. It's kind of noisy, a lot noisier than it was in the old days, according to Dad. "Back then a library meant you were working quietly." But it's warm today, and the library's air-conditioned and free, so I can see why everyone would want to come here. A lot of places in San Diego don't have air-conditioning because, also in the Old Days According to Dad, it didn't used to get so hot and humid. Climate change.

I wipe the sweat off my forehead and look around. Half of me hopes Ty won't show up. He'll argue with me and nothing's going to get done. Maybe I should just leave and be the one who doesn't show. But that's not me.

Plus, at that moment I see him wave from the end of a long, crowded table. I wonder if he has to wait a long time to use a computer. "Hey," he says to the floor. There are no open seats nearby, so I can't sit down.

I nod. It's hard to talk if I think someone really doesn't like me. It's as if my body actually physically decides not to respond.

Finally he glances up, his expression like someone just farted in his face. He stands. "It's crowded in here. Let's go to the park." He starts moving.

I just walked *through* the park, I want to point out, but instead I nod again.

"What are you, a bobblehead?" Ty pushes the door open. He doesn't even make sure it stays that way when I walk out, and I have to make sure it doesn't shut on me.

I trudge across the wide lawn behind the community pool, following Ty across the street and back to the park. The shadiest tables are taken.

Now I'm breathing a little hard. The humidity makes my heart feel like it's having trouble pumping. I need to sit. I need shade.

Ty heads toward a sunny concrete picnic bench, but I finally speak up. "Let's go under the tree."

"On the grass?" He wrinkles his nose. "Dogs pee on grass."

Dogs probably peed everywhere in this park at some point. I want to tell him that's why we wear clothes, but instead I stay silent and go under one of the huge trees and sit down, cross-legged. Ty sits across from me. I open my Chromebook, hoping we don't have to look up anything on the internet. Because there's zero Wi-Fi out here. My back prickles with sweat. I realize I drank my whole water bottle during class and didn't refill it.

"Can I ask you a question?"

A twinge of annoyance goes through me, the same as when Luke's being a pain, and I spit out the kind of answer I'd give my brother. "You just did."

Ty blinks in surprise at this unexpected reply. He huffs. "You know that's not what I mean."

I shrug yet again, wiping my forehead with my forearm. I don't know what he wants from me. What have I ever done to him?

He cocks his head. "Why do you think you're better than everyone else?"

My spine stiffens. What's he talking about? I think I'm worse than everyone else, if anything. How could he possibly think that? I swallow. "I . . . I don't." I focus really hard on the Chromebook. We need to write this thing. It's due in two weeks, but we have to show an outline, then a rough draft, and then do edits, and we're going to have to do a presentation. Which we have to practice first. So we're definitely heading to an F right now. I want to say all this to him, but my stupid words are gumming up.

I start sweating even more. What is his problem with me, exactly?

"Well, you act like you do." Ty's stomach growls loudly. I have a bag of Cheez-Its in my backpack, and I take it out and hold it across the grass to him. He looks at it as if I've offered him a plateful of ants.

I force myself to take several deep breaths, fighting the urge to get up and run away. Or to put my head down and cover my face with my hair. Instead I sink down a little deeper into myself. I want to answer him, if only so we can finish this stupid project.

I look at the very green grass, the trees. My mind flashes to Miss Gwen. Being in this moment. Reading your partner's emotions. Let yourself feel the energy your partner's giving off.

I look at Ty, try to figure out what he's thinking. Does it matter? He's practically vibrating hostility as he gnaws on his pencil and squints at me. Disdain is another, like he thinks I'm just about the lowliest person he's ever met. "You never talk. You're the only one who gets to leave class and let the teacher read your stuff. Why do you get special treatment?" Ty pulls out some clumps of grass. "It's not fair."

So I was right about the emotions, at least. I swallow, my throat scratchy. He doesn't know me. I want to tell him so, calmly, but the words still won't come out, all jumbled together where the scratchiness is.

"Answer me." Ty raises his voice so loud that someone walking by looks over. I sink lower into myself. "Sheesh, you're such a snob."

I am not, I want to yell.

And suddenly my body does something new. It unfreezes.

Blood rushes into my neck and my heart thumps harder. My ears are filled with nothing but the sound of my heart beating like the taiko drum Jīchan plays. BAM BAM BAM BAM. It thrums in my jaw, on the roof of my mouth.

Mom says adrenaline is what makes you have the flight-or-fight thing. I can't fight Ty and I'm not going to just run away from him. So instead it feels as if someone's just mixed baking soda and vinegar together in my veins. A volcano erupting.

Ty stares at me hard, his face reddening. "Or maybe you're a robot?"

I don't say anything.

He squints. "Though you look kind of mad now," he says triumphantly. "Finally, the robot reacts."

I ignore him. I need to calm myself down. Maybe that's why I always freeze, so this doesn't happen. I try to take a deep breath. *Notice your surroundings.* I stare at the white flowers growing out of the grass, picking one up and holding it to my nose. It smells like cut grass. My nose itches.

Still my blood crashes through my body. I close my eyes. *These are five things you find in the park. Dogs, one. People, two. Ty, three.* I try to swallow, but something sticks in my throat.

"See, you're not even answering me." Ty sags back. "That's just rude."

I don't owe you an answer. I don't owe you anything, I want to shout, the kind of thing Mom would say. But I'm too hot. I lose track of my thoughts. I close the Chromebook and hug it to my chest, which makes the ICD press into my muscles in a strange, comforting way. I'm sweating now, and my stomach rears up like an angry horse.

"Ava?" Ty sounds like he's moved away from me. "Hey—are you okay?"

Sick, I try to say, but I don't, and I put my hand on the ground and lean over, getting ready to barf.

But then something strange happens.

My heart—pauses. Then it flutters, as if there's a hummingbird in my chest, its wings beating very softly and fast. Now the blood-rushing feeling is done, but it's too—too light. I put two fingers on my neck, checking my pulse.

Dum. Dum. Pause. *Du—m. Dumdumdum.* Pause. *Dum.*

It speeds up, but still with that pause, as if the hummingbird's trying its best to break out. Now it feels like there's bread stuck in my throat, too. I cough, then cough again. Sweat breaks out on my forehead, under my armpits, on my chest. My fingers grab through the sharp pricks of the grass, dirt wedging under my nails, but I barely feel it and I don't care.

What's going on?

There's a sharp burning sensation in my chest. Tears come into my eyes. Am I going to get shocked, the big kind? The worry makes me anxious, and the anxiety makes the heart worse. A lose-lose situation.

I try to take a big breath but I can't. I need to calm down right now. I lie down on the grass, so if I do get shocked and pass out, I won't get hurt by falling. I'm proud of myself for remembering that.

"There's something wrong with her!" I hear Ty say. He sounds like he's on the other side of the world. "Somebody help!"

That flapping feeling continues and then my chest burns again, all hot inside, as if I ate a bunch of spicy food an hour ago. Only for a couple seconds. Then the feeling goes away. I recognize the feeling from the doctor's office when they test the pacemaker by making it give me a tiny shock. I'm getting paced.

It will give me three different small shocks to pace me. If that doesn't work, if my heart still beats wrong, the ICD will take over and give me a big shock. "You probably won't feel it," the doctor told me, "because people usually pass out before that. But if you do, it feels like a punch in the chest."

Which didn't make me feel better then, and doesn't now, either, when the memory flashes in front of me like the doctor's here right now, telling me that.

Fear crowds out every other antianxiety exercise I've ever learned. I try to concentrate on anything else but all I can think about is the fact that I'm going to pass out. I'm about to get kicked in the chest. I'm breathing too shallowly, my stomach moving in and out faster and faster. I can't get air into my lungs.

I curl into a ball on the ground, still breathing wrong, almost as if I'm hiccupping without hiccups. Something scratches my face, my arm. For a second, I think I'm in bed. Like I'm about to fall asleep, and I struggle not to.

"Ava!" It's not Ty's voice, but Luke's. My brother leans over me, his face silhouetted against the waving leaves. "Ava, take deep breaths." His voice is lower than usual, commanding as Dad's. But I can't. He takes my hand and squeezes it. "Purse your lips and pretend you're blowing out birthday candles."

I do what he says. I try to imagine a cake with candles, but what I see instead is a hummingbird. Sitting on the branch of the orchid tree, oddly, unnaturally frozen in sleep.

And then everything goes black.

CHAPTER 28

I open my eyes to my brother's creased and red face. "Ava, Ava, are you all right? You got shocked, I think. You passed out. You were flailing around."

I put my hand on my ICD pacemaker. It's the same as always. Hard, but not doing anything. "I didn't feel it," I murmur, glad for this. Because it's supposed to feel like a donkey kick. But I'm sore, as though I knocked into something with my chest, and I feel like I've been asleep for a long time and am having trouble waking up. "I'm all right."

"I need someone to call 911," Luke says to the gathering crowd of grown-ups. Just like we learned in that CPR class my parents made us take. "I've got you, I've got you," he murmurs over and over, and I realize he's cradling me in his lap. He's warm and solid and I'm safe. Finally I start to relax.

Sirens blare and firefighter paramedics in dark blue

uniforms are suddenly hovering over me, lifting me onto a stretcher, wheeling me into the ambulance. Lucky for me, the fire station is just a few blocks away. All around kids and grown-ups watch. Some are actually crying, though I'm the one in trouble, and I don't want them to be scared. "I'm okay," I try to tell them, but my voice comes out really quiet.

It might have been cool to sit by the ambulance driver because they turn on the sirens and we go through several red lights, but I'm on a bed in the back. Luke's up front. The paramedics stick a funny-smelling oxygen tube into my nose, which is actually okay with me because the ambulance smells like antiseptic, like a hospital. "I think she's just dehydrated," the paramedic says. She looks barely older than Hudson. "Her heart's beating completely normally."

"It's not normal." Luke turns to say this. "She's got something called noncompaction cardiomyopathy. Look it up."

"Simmer down, kiddo," the other, older paramedic says.

"I've never heard of it," the younger one mumbles. "I don't see anything wrong here."

"Why do you think she's got an ICD? Because she likes it?" Luke explodes. "Call Dr. White at Children's."

"Is she taking any medications?" the older one says, and Luke tells him. Now the younger one's looking the disease up on her phone and murmuring, "Ohhhhh—that's not good. Poor thing." And pats my leg. Which makes me feel zero percent better.

But I'm glad that Luke's here, making sure I'm okay. Even though my brother and I don't always get along, I guess this proves that he'll show up when it counts. And that he has my back.

They take us to Children's, and the ER doctor has also never heard of what I have because nobody's heard of it unless they're a cardiologist, and everyone's freaking out thinking I'm an eleven-year-old having a heart attack. It's not until my grandparents arrive that things start calming down. "Dr. White's in surgery but he'll be here as soon as he can," Nana Linda tells me. I'm in a room now, dressed in one of those cotton robes with cartoon tigers printed on it, and they've stuck an IV in my arm, which pinches and pulls. And I'm covered in stickers and wires for the heart monitor, plus a blood pressure cuff. Very Frankenstein—and not very comfortable.

Jīchan's face looks like it went from being a Shiba Inu puppy to a Shar-Pei because of me. I know he's having flashbacks to my grandmother's illness. Seeing him worried is the thing that hurts me the most. He wipes tears out of his eyes.

"I'm sorry, Jīchan. I'm okay." I try to sit up, but the wires hold me down. I push the button on the bed to raise the back. "See? I'm fine."

"You're so brave, Ava." Now his face is completely wet, and this makes my tears start, too.

What he doesn't know is I'm not brave at all. I was afraid the whole time.

I think back to Luke complaining that I don't deal with the real world. Well, I guess I can if I have to. But I didn't exactly have a choice in whether or not I dealt with this. I sniffle, shake my head. Nana Linda hands both me and my grandfather tissues and we blow our noses.

"That sounds like a snot duet," Luke says from his corner.

It does. I laugh a little. "Gross." My brother looks like he's just been in a fight and he's waiting in the principal's office. His hair's sticking up and the neck of his T-shirt is all stretched out—I wonder if I pulled on it. Luke's face is pale and streaked with dirt as he holds it in his hands. I want to hug him, but that's so not his style.

Jīchan pats my hand. "Your parents are on their way. How are you feeling?"

I take in a deep breath. Nothing hurts. I didn't feel the actual shock, so that's good. But I wouldn't mind going home and getting into my own bed and sleeping for a couple days. "I'm better."

Luke leans forward, his forehead creased. "That

kid you were with was bawling. He kept saying, 'I'm so sorry.' Who was that?"

"Ty. From my English class. That thing Hudson was helping me with." I turn my head. I'm tired, but otherwise feeling okay.

"Well, if he's mean, you don't need to be working with him." Luke points at me as if I'd chosen a mean partner on purpose. "You don't need that kind of stress."

I blink slowly at him, remembering all the times he hasn't really understood my anxiety. "I thought I would just be tough. Like you told me."

Luke opens and closes his mouth. He looks at the floor before meeting my eyes. "I'm sorry, Ava. I didn't really understand."

Maybe Ty doesn't, either. I smile a little at my brother, forgiving him. "Just don't tell me to *get over it* again and we'll be good." I hold up my hand and he pops over to high-five it.

"Ava Andrews. Why, I wasn't expecting you to visit for another year!" Dr. White sticks his head in. He's got silver hair and a twinkly grandpa manner. He picks up my chart. "Let's just see what in doodly-doo we have here."

Luke and I roll our eyes. That kind of thing used to be funny when we were little, but we grew out of it. My brothers used to see Dr. White, too, until we had genetic testing and found my brothers didn't have the gene. My mom has it, but her heart's healthy. This thing is weird like that—you can have spongy tissue and a normal-beating heart, or it can be sick. Some people have to take medication; some don't. You can live to be ninety years old or die suddenly when you're young.

Suddenly I'm really, really glad I have the defibrillator.

Dr. White notices him. "Hey, there, Luka-reeno. You've grown a foot or two since I last laid eyes on you."

Luke crosses his arms. Grunts.

Dr. White turns to me. "Good news. Your device worked. Your heart's nice and steady now." He asks what I was doing before that.

I tell him the story.

He sits. "I think you might have had a panic attack first. Panic attacks might lead to arrhythmias, this heart stuff, in a condition like yours."

No joke, I think. I exchange a glance with Luke. He rolls his eyes in our shared *These adults!* language.

"Are you still going to therapy?" Dr. White asks. "It's not good to bottle up your feelings."

"It's not?" Luke asks. "Doesn't it make stuff . . . easier?"

"You're the bottler, Luke. And no, it's not good to push all your feelings down." I roll my eyes again, this time alone. Mom and Dad have been trying to get Luke to express himself forever, but ever since he became a teenager he's pretty much closed up like an oyster. "I think about my emotions all the time. Like, twenty-four/seven."

"Maybe that's part of the problem." Dr. White writes something down.

I know that's part of the problem. Lots of things are part of my problem. Mr. Matt's always talking to my parents about "building up Ava's tolerance for emotional discomfort."

My body's acting as though I just ran a marathon. I gulp down the juice box someone brought me earlier. Then I burp loud, like Luke. It's impressive, echoing off the hard surfaces in the room, and it lasts and lasts and lasts.

I don't even say excuse me.

The room goes quiet, all of them eyeing me. "What?" I say.

Luke holds out his fist. "Good one, Ava." I bump it.

"I see you're getting over your shyness." Dr. White ruffles my hair, messing it up, then holds up his stethoscope. "Mind if I take a listen?"

After some other tests, during which the rest of my family shows up, Dr. White clears me to go, telling me to stay hydrated, manage my anxiety, rest, and all that. "I may try a beta-blocker next time," he tells my parents, "but last time we did that, it dropped her blood pressure too low."

A beta-blocker is a kind of medicine that basically

would kill off any anxiety I have and keep adrenaline out of my system. But I tried one before and I got so tired I couldn't get out of bed. It was awful.

"She was doing so well," Mom says, her voice icicled with sadness. I grab her hand and squeeze it, but there's nothing I can say to make her feel better. She strokes my hair with her other hand.

At home Mom and Dad tuck me in. Even though it's warm, Mom's changed into her plushy Chewbacca pajama onesie with the hood on because she knows it makes me smile. "Aowo-rrrrrrr," she says in Chewbacca voice, from the back of her throat. She gives me a kiss on the forehead, then both cheeks, like she did when I was very small.

"Good night to you, too, Wookiee." I hug her close for a moment. She feels like a warm stuffed animal.

Speaking of which, there are about thirty toys on my feet, and Dad grunts as he moves them aside to sit. "Which one do you want?"

I point to the unicorn with dirty white fur. Diamond the unicorn. I've had it since I was four. He pretends like it's racing up to me and I grab it.

"I want you to relax for a day," Mom says. "We'll Netflix-binge." She kisses my forehead again. "I'll take tomorrow off."

"You don't have to." Mom never takes a day off.

"I want to." She smiles, and pain flashes through her

eyes. "I'm sorry I wasn't here."

I grab her hand. The worst part of everything is having people worry about me. "Nobody can be with me all the time, Mom."

"I know. But if I could, I'd follow you around like Chewbacca followed Han Solo." She squishes her face in an exaggerated smile and I imitate her.

Dad squeezes my shoulder in his Dad way. "I'm glad you're okay."

"I would hope so." I turn onto my side. "I'm your only daughter."

Mom and Dad snort. "I'll leave the door cracked." She turns off the light.

"Dr. White said I'm fine," I call after them.

I lie awake, clutching my stuffed animal. Dr. White said my anxiety had a not-small role to play in this thing. Apparently I still don't have that under control. Though I'm trying. I'm doing therapy. Am I not trying hard enough?

Maybe I do bottle things up. I wish I'd been able to just tell Ty what I was thinking. Even telling him to be quiet would've been better than nothing.

I slip out of bed and get the phone off my desk. It's after eleven back east. Mom told me that she'd texted Zelia's mom, but Zelia hasn't texted me. Almost automatically, I start typing a message to her. But really—she should reach out to me. Right?

I delete the message. Instead, I text the improv group. *So a funny thing happened after school. I'm okay now.* I explain briefly.

Texts shoot back.

OMG! says Ryan. *That's crazy.*

You should have come to Fosters Freeze, Chad says.

Did Ty do this to you??? Cecily says.

Totally horrible! Babel says.

Glad you're not dead, Jonathan says. This makes me smile.

Through the door I hear Luke's voice from the living room. "I was so scared."

"You did great," Dad says.

There's an unfamiliar noise, like a dog whining in a closed room. I creep toward the door and listen. It's Luke. I haven't heard him cry since he was like eight and he broke his leg while he was skateboarding. Even though the bone was trying to push through his skin, he didn't bawl—he just cried silently.

A strange sort of ache shakes through me.

Luke was scared. That means—it must mean—he loves me. I mean, I always kind of knew he did, and he sort of has to because I'm his sister. But he's never acted like it, the way Hudson does. Until today.

This makes me feel so warm and squishy inside that I want to hug Luke tight, but he doesn't like that kind of thing. So I get up and go out to the living room. Dad's patting Luke on the back. "What are you doing out of bed, Ava?"

I sit down on Dad's other side. "I'm sorry for what happened."

"It's not your fault," Dad and Luke say at the same time.

"Still." I hand a box of tissues to Luke. He takes one, honks his nose, doesn't look at me.

"It's not your fault, either, Luke."

He shrugs. "I don't know why I'm crying so hard."

"You had to hold it together until we got home. It happens." Mom appears with a mug of hot chocolate. She sets it on the table in front of him, then sits down next to me, her arm around my shoulders. Almost the whole family's wedged onto the couch.

"Where's Hudson?" I ask.

"Here." Hudson appears. "You think I can't hear when there's hot chocolate going on?" He squishes himself into the couch and it's just like it was when we were very small, cuddling with Mom and Dad. Except with a lot more body odor.

"What happened, exactly?" Mom strokes my hair. "I didn't hear the whole story."

I take a shaky breath and start talking. I know they're exchanging glances above my head. Like *Can you believe Ava?* To hear me retell the story, it all sounds silly, like I should have never been upset to begin with.

"I don't know why, but it felt like me and Ty were samurai sword fighting."

"It's your fight or flight or freeze. You feel things more than average," Mom says.

"Still. He should have left her alone." Luke gulps down most of his drink, leaving a chocolate mustache.

"Sometimes when you don't talk much people get the wrong idea. They think you're stuck-up or you don't care." Dad looks thoughtful.

"That's not fair." I point at my face. "This is just how I look. Why do people assume they know what I'm thinking?"

Mom smiles. "I remember one time when I was a new mother; Hudson was four months old. I was almost done with the shopping and he just started bawling. He wasn't dirty, wasn't hungry. I decided to get in line as fast as I could. Well, some lady started glaring at me."

I imagine this like I was there, and it makes me angry. "That's not nice."

"I snapped at her, 'Haven't you ever seen a baby crying before?' and she looked so startled," Mom says. "She said, 'I was honestly just trying to add up my grocery bill.' Then I realized she hadn't been glaring at me—I happened to look at *her* while she was frowning and then she made eye contact." She shakes her head. "You're right, nobody knows what you're thinking. And what other people think is none of your business. So what if people think you're snobby because you're quiet? That's on them."

"Besides," Hudson adds, "most people are thinking about themselves. Not about you."

"Yeah, I'm thinking about myself like ninety-nine percent of the time," Luke says.

"Tell us something we don't know." Hudson gives Luke a gentle kick with the side of his foot.

Maybe that's true, but it doesn't make things easier with Ty. I blow out a breath. "My project's still not done."

"You can ask for an extension," Dad says. "You still want to work with that kid?"

I shrug. It's not like Ty did it on purpose. I mean, I get into arguments all the time with my brothers and my heart's fine during those.

I think it was a mess of everything else that was happening. Ty and the library. Navegando Point. The heat. Fighting with Zelia.

"No, she doesn't," Luke says.

That pushes me into a decision. Luke means well, but he's not going to tell me what to do. Neither is Ty.

I don't think Ty's bad, I really don't. He and I don't understand each other, is the problem.

Cecily said that Ryan used to be a bully, until he did improv and learned that other people have feelings. Ty just doesn't seem to get my point of view. I want one more try to make him understand. "That's up to me."

I struggle out of the comfy couch. "I'm going to make myself a hot chocolate. Anyone else want anything?"

"I'll make you one." Mom gets up, but I'm already moving.

"It's not like it's hard. It's a packet." I go in the kitchen first. I need to show them I'm fine, just fine, not a porcelain doll that's been glued back together.

I'm strong. I'm mostly normal. And I want to be regular, forever. I want to do what I want to do without feeling so awful. My napkin project. Getting along with difficult kids. Cotillion. Going to Maine. Improv. Protesting Navegando Point.

I go back to my room and grab a notebook. I have ideas, and I need to write them down.

CHAPTER 29

D r. White says I can go back to school in a week, so I spend the rest of the days hanging out at home. Cecily, Ryan, and Chad all come over after school on Wednesday and we watch She-Ra together, settling on the couch with a big bowl of popcorn. "Ty's been out of school all week," Cecily tells me, and I wonder if it's because of what happened.

If I were him, I'd feel really bad. Not to mention anxious.

I find myself hoping Ty's okay. That he just developed a cold and that's why he's out.

Zelia texts me while we're watching She-Ra. *Are you okay? Your mom told my mom everything.*

She's probably feeling a little guilty, like Ty. Maybe not that bad, but kind of. I glance up at my friends. These are the people who are here, right now. They keep their word. They wouldn't just throw me under the bus for summer camp like Zelia did.

Maybe, after our last conversation, I don't want to talk to her.

Ryan nudges me. "You're missing the good part!"

I put away my phone.

My parents fuss over me all week, and on Thursday, Dad takes me to see Mr. Matt. He gives me a sympathetic pat on the shoulder. "I'm so glad you're okay."

"I'm fine." I look at the Halloween decorations in his office. Lots of coloring-book pumpkins—they must be from his other patients.

I walk over to the window and look down at the stream. There's so much swirling around inside me, like sand churned up by ocean waves. I'm not sure where to start. Should I tell him about how mean Zelia was? About Ty? About how Luke actually loves me or how I found out my friends were there for me?

It's too much to think about, let alone talk about. If I start talking, those waves will take over. I might start crying. So I'm quiet.

"Tell me what it was like," Mr. Matt prompts. "You must have been scared."

I count three turtles today, thinking back to being in the ambulance and then in the hospital. "I wasn't scared at the time," I say finally. "I was getting through it."

"That's normal."

I flop down into the chair. If I don't think about this,

I won't start bawling. "I'm barely freaking out at all." Ever since I've been home, I've had people around me. I haven't been alone at all. Maybe that's why. "I'm *processing* it all very well." Ha. I've used his own words. I grin at him, pretending I'm a character in a spy movie who fights a bunch of people without breaking a sweat.

Mr. Matt grins back. "Good use of the word, Ava." He shifts. "Honestly, if I were you, I'd be freaking out a lot."

Suddenly the wave comes for me. I grab a tissue from the box he keeps nearby and wipe my eyes.

"It's okay to cry," Mr. Matt says.

I was acting like Luke had, being fake-cool. I was bottling. Mr. Matt's right—I need to get it out. I nod, more tears already coming, and this time I don't try to stop them. "I thought I was going to die," I admit. "And I couldn't stop it." A sob escapes me, and it sounds kind of like the one Luke let out. Maybe there's some particular sound of crying that runs in our family.

"But you didn't." Mr. Matt gets up and pours water from a cooler into a cup. He hands it to me.

I blow my nose, then drink. The tears stop. "Yeah. I'm here." I pick up the stress ball, considering. Dr. White always told me that the ICD was only there to protect me, like having my own personal medical crew with me at all times. He said that actually I'm safer than most people. "It could have been worse. Like if I didn't have the ICD. That would have been really bad."

It reminds me of what Dad says sometimes when people complain about getting old: "It's better than the alternative."

I'd rather have the ICD than not be here at all.

"It did its job. It kept you safe," Mr. Matt says.

With that realization, a kind of calm comes over me, and the mix of thoughts settle like sand in water. I put down the stress ball and blow out a breath. The thought I want to talk about is Zelia. But that will set me off again, and I'm feeling as raw as a new sunburn.

Instead I talk about someone else. "There's this kid who's been my project partner." This is the first time I've really volunteered anything without Mr. Matt prompting me. Maybe it's just taken me a whole year to get that comfortable with him.

Or maybe it's that I'm getting more comfortable with myself.

Mr. Matt sits back in his chair. "Tell me about him."

I spill the whole story from the beginning. How Ty thought I was snooty. Our fights. The vice principal. The shock incident. How I want to work with him anyway.

"It's interesting that you still want to give him another chance after all that's happened." Mr. Matt chews on his pen.

"I just don't think he really understood me." I imagine how I look to other people. How other people look to me. What do I really know about Ty? Do I know if *he* has any invisible disabilities? For all I know, he does. A twinge of guilt vibrates in my stomach. I made assumptions about him just like he made about me. "Maybe I could've tried harder to understand him, too."

Mr. Matt nods. "That's very mature of you, Ava."

"Thanks." I smile at Mr. Matt, for once taking the compliment instead of trying to hide from it. I'm not actually trying to be mature. I'm just trying to do what feels right to me. I look at the turtles again.

Now maybe I can bring up Zelia without falling apart. I turn back to Mr. Matt, but he's putting away his clipboard. "That's our time for today," he says with a smile. And I have to admit, I'm a little relieved.

At lunch on Monday, I walk out into the courtyard with my lunch. Then I hear my name, a thing that hasn't happened since Zelia left. "Ava!" Cecily's waving from under the lunch arbor. Ryan and Chad sit across from her.

I walk over. "What's up?"

"You're here!" Chad leaps over and bear-hugs me. The others join in until we're having a group hug. We rock back and forth for a minute. Their faces are right next to mine, and I can smell the onion Cecily ate on her sandwich and the ranch Doritos on Ryan's breath, plus their varying stinky smells since we all had PE this morning—but I don't mind. Not one bit.

I close my eyes. It's so nice to be part of a group. I always thought that Zelia gave me everything I needed, but maybe asking her to be everything was too much. These kids all give me different things. Cecily's steady. Ryan shows me a different point of view. And Chad is just plain fun.

"No PDA!" some grown-up lunch monitor yells.

"This isn't PDA!" Ryan protests, and we giggle and step back from each other. "Sheesh. Can't even hug your friends these days."

I check my phone the way I often do at lunch. There's a text from Mom. *Hope you have a great day. Love you.* A text from Dad saying the same thing. A text from Hudson offering to pick me up after school.

A text from Zelia.

Ava, I know you're okay because my mom talked to your mom. I know you hate me. But I want to talk to you. Call me?

My throat gets a lump.

Cecily notices my expression. "Everything okay?"

"Yeah." I nod, put away the phone. If Zelia's only going to be nice to me because she feels bad that I was sick, then I don't want to be her friend. "Everything's fine."

We sit down at the table and I unwrap my almond butter and jelly sandwich, ignoring the butterflies that come up when I think about my idea. It's okay. They're baby butterflies. "I've been thinking about what else we can do besides the flyers."

Chad wrinkles his nose. "That was a disaster."

"What if . . . ?" I swallow some water to help me get these next words out because half of me can't believe I'm saying them. But we already did it at Fosters Freeze, so will it really be so bad? I remember what Luke said, about how I need to deal with the real world. This is the real world, isn't it? I mean, organizing a protest isn't just like walking down the street. It's like poking a bear. "What if we do an improv show down there? Maybe with the grown-up teams. Show everyone what will be missing if Navegando Point goes away."

"That's a great idea!" Ryan exclaims.

"You're not just *yes, and*–ing me, are you?" I close my eyes.

"No, Ava. It is a good idea and we should ask Miss Gwen about it right now." Cecily takes out her phone.

I look at their lit-up faces and how they're practically rubbing their hands together with excitement and realize I didn't have to second-guess myself. I *do* have good ideas. I can do things. All of them.

"Saturday after class, then," I say to Cecily, and she puts that in the email.

Ty's been absent since I got back, so we can't work on our project. I hope Luke didn't scare him into changing schools or something.

Mr. Sukow takes me aside during class on Tuesday. "How are you doing, Ava?"

"I'm okay." Today I look directly at him, not at his nose or his hairline. Maybe that shock scared away some of my nervousness around him.

His face is all scrunched up with concern and maybe guilt. He had to have known Ty and I didn't get along, right? I mean, anyone with two okay-working eyes would see that. But maybe he's got so many students he doesn't pay attention to each relationship.

"I'm going to give you extra time for your project. You want to work on it alone?" His brow furrows with concern, and it makes me feel squirmy inside. Is this the kind of special treatment that Ty was talking about? Why should I be the only one who does a solo project?

I chew my lip. It would be so easy to knock out this project all by myself. It probably wouldn't have to be that great.

But avoiding people hasn't worked. Not talking to people hasn't gotten me what I wanted. Staying quiet never got me what I really needed, either.

I suck in air, look Mr. Sukow in the eye. "Is he actually sick?" I ask Mr. Sukow. "Or is he staying home because of what happened to me?"

Mr. Sukow crosses his arms. "I don't know for sure, but my guess is probably more of the latter."

I should be glad he's not here, but I'm not. He didn't know doing that would hurt me. My throat aches a little, thinking about Ty sitting at home. I wonder if he cried like Luke did. If anyone made him hot chocolate.

Ty and I don't have to be friends. We just have to work on this paper napkin project. And I want to tell Ty about me. I want him to understand.

Suddenly I know what to do. "Can I get his homework packet?" I ask. "I'll take it to him."

CHAPTER 30

Nana Linda finds Ty's mom's number in the school directory and calls her, simply saying I want to drop off his homework. Then, later in the afternoon, she drives me over there. He lives in an apartment building behind a gas station on a busy street, kind of far from the school. It would probably take him an hour to walk home, and more than that to get to school—it's all uphill.

As I get out of the car, the rush hour traffic honks and revs, and it makes my insides itch. I'm glad we live in a quieter area that's not so crowded. I wonder if we lived here, if I'd be even more anxious. Or if I'd learn how to deal.

We walk up a narrow, winding concrete path past two-story brown apartments. The kitchen windows all open to the courtyard, and people move around inside. From the windows come all kinds of different dinner scents: hamburgers and roasting vegetables and Mexican food spices and other spices I've never smelled before. There's a happy, busy hum that we don't have on our street, where most of the living spaces and windows are in the back, where the street can't see.

Nana Linda rings their doorbell. "I'm going to let you do the talking, sweetie."

I nod.

Ty opens the door. Through the metal security screen, I can barely make out his face, but I do see his eyes are huge. "Ava?"

"Let them in, Ty," a woman says from behind him. Ty undoes the lock and swings the door open.

I step onto a worn carpet with a lot of stains. Ty shoves his hands into his pockets and shuffles aside, staring at the floor.

"Hi. I'm Liz. Thanks so much for bringing Ty his homework." Her shoulders slump forward. "We don't have internet quite just yet, so we can't get it from the website." She's wearing a Denny's waitress uniform, and I wonder if she's on her way to work or just getting home, or both, since Ty said she had two jobs. She looks familiar—I must have seen her at school.

I look around. There's a wide-screen TV set on a bookcase filled with a gaming console and an old encyclopedia set. Two stacks of library books sit beside it. There's a small sectional sofa and a small dining table for two. It all looks like it came from IKEA. I wonder if

Ty loves IKEA as much as I do.

She invites us to sit down, and Nana Linda turns around two dining room chairs for us as Ty and his mom take the couch. The sofa's really only big enough for three if they sit close together, and I guess Nana Linda doesn't want to squeeze into personal space.

Liz sits next to Ty, her back straight, as though she's trying not to mess up her uniform. She looks both younger than my mom and older, too. She pats Ty's knee. "He's feeling much better today, aren't you?"

He nods, staring ahead. I don't think he's told her about what happened to me. I mean, I guess there was no reason to. I open up my folder and get out his homework sheets. "Here. Mr. Sukow says it's due Friday."

He takes it without a word and sets it on the coffee table.

My whole body clenches like a jar that's impossible to open.

"Well." Liz looks at me and then at Ty. "Would you like something to drink?"

"Some water would be lovely." Nana Linda stands. "I'll help you." She retreats into the kitchen space with Liz.

I shift in my chair, my heart pounding. Now I have two choices. I could let things be. Or I could try to change things. I didn't come here to do nothing. Maybe I'll make things worse—but how much worse could they really get?

242

Ty's still staring at the floor. I clear my throat and look around the room. There's a laundry basket filled with clothes. On top is a T-shirt that says *NAVEGANDO POINT CUPCAKES*. "Hey. I like that place." I point.

"Liked, I guess. It's gone, did you know?"

"I know. My mom worked there." Ty's mouth turned down.

"Oh!" I look over at Ty's mom. She was working when Dad and I bought all those cupcakes—that's why she looks familiar. And that's why Ty had a cupcake. "I saw her there. That was one of my favorite stores. I'm really sorry." I remember what Ryan told me about his bullying days, about how he had some stuff going on. Ty's got some stuff going on, too.

He gives me a one-shouldered shrug. "It's not a big deal," he mutters. "Not compared to what happened to you."

Oh. Now's a good time to say this. "I wanted to tell you that what happened to me wasn't your fault."

His jaw clenches and he blinks like an owl. Then, slowly, he lifts his head and makes eye contact.

I continue. "I have this heart condition. It was a lot of different stuff."

We're silent for a moment. Then Ty says, almost without moving his mouth, "I'm sorry."

I nod at him, waiting for him to keep going.

"I wanted to stay, but your brother told me to get lost." He grimaces. "I'm really glad you're okay." Ty crosses his arms, crunches his legs in. "I shouldn't have . . ." He trails off. "I shouldn't have assumed things about you."

"Like what?" I want him to say the things out loud.

"Like that you're snobby, or spoiled. Or quiet."

I throw up my hands. "Quiet shouldn't be a negative word, you know. It means I'm *thinking*." I shake my head. "My mom says if your lips are moving, you're not listening."

His eyebrows are practically touching his hairline. "Those are the most words I've ever heard you say."

I lift my chin, pretending to be tough. "Better get used to it." I'm feeling lighter. As if I might be able to be comfortable around him. "I should have told you from the beginning how I felt, but I was afraid."

"You?" Ty's eyes widen. "You were afraid of me?"

I nod.

He gives a small, disbelieving laugh. "Nobody's ever afraid of me. I'm just the little smart aleck in the back." Ty smiles. "I guess . . . I was actually kinda afraid of you. I thought you were always judging me or something."

"Totally not. Well, not usually." We both laugh. I shrug because I'm not sure what else to say. "Anyway. You might be more afraid of me now that I talk to you. You released the kraken."

He snorts, then smiles a little. "I can't wait to see what that looks like."

* * *

Nana Linda and I say goodbye to Ty and his mom, then follow the path back out to the car. It's twilight now, and the apartments are filled with dishes clinking, people talking, and kitchen lights shining through windows.

Some people stand on the path, smoking, and Nana Linda steers me wide around them since smoke makes my chest ache. I would have a hard time living here.

I think about how where I was born and where I live had nothing to do with me. It had to do with the fact that Jīchan and Obāchan just happened to buy a house here a long time ago, when it was cheaper, and raised Mom in this area, so she grew to love it. And that Mom and Dad had families who supported them through college, and that they also bought the house a while ago, before prices went sky-high.

It's so weird to think about luck like that. I could have just as easily been born into another family, in another country. Not been me at all.

"Penny for your thoughts?" Nana Linda says.

I open the car door. "It'll be more like a quarter."

Nana Linda drives me home. "Did your talk go well?"

"Yeah. I think we're okay." I remember how I talked to Ty. How I acted like I was in an improv scene, kind of, when I told him what I thought.

I turn to face her. "Nana, do you think if I pretend to be tough, then I'm only fake tough?"

"No." Nana Linda reaches over and pats my knee. "You're just calling on an inner strength, Ava. Everybody's afraid. Courage is driving right through the fear."

Maybe being brave isn't about not being scared. It could be about dealing with something you can't change, like my heart. Or it could be about deciding something's important enough to you to face being afraid for a little bit. Like with me and Ty.

She shakes her head. "I used to be afraid all the time, but I just got on with things."

"Of what?" I can't imagine this.

"Well, when I liked your grandfather." She blushes. "We had been spending time together as friends. I knew I liked him but I thought he just needed someone to talk to. And your grandmother hadn't been gone too long. But one day I told him that I thought he was a wonderful man."

"And that did it?" I'd never heard this story.

"No, your grandfather didn't get the hint. What did it was when I went on a date with another man, and then he realized he wanted to be the one doing that." Nana Linda smiles.

"And the rest is history." A burbling fountain erupts inside me, and both of us start giggling. For no particular reason at all.

CHAPTER 31

We walk into Navegando Point with Miss Gwen, Nana Linda, Dad, and Ryan's dad behind us. Ryan's dad has a professional camera with a long microphone on it. We find a spot on the grass between a juggler and a tarot card reader, next to the concrete path and the short seawall, and get in a circle. People keep stopping to take photos of the boats in the harbor and the Coronado Bridge in the distance. On the grass, families picnic. Little kids run around shouting. Along the edge, entertainers perform. A woman ties some long yellow balloons into a wiener dog for a little kid. A few people search the ground with metal detectors, looking for loose change and I don't know what. It's a Saturday, so it's crowded, with everyone gathering around the juggler. A cool breeze lifts up off the water, feeling nice on my sweaty scalp.

I see Becca standing with her mom, Mrs. Ladigan.

They're both wearing flowered sundresses. "Hey!" Becca gives me a hug, which surprises me but makes me feel welcome. "You look so pretty! That's a great color on you."

I tug on the collar of my turquoise shirt. "Um, thanks. So do you."

She smiles and I introduce her to the others. Becca's turning out to be nice, now that I'm getting to know her. I wonder if she thinks that about me. I hope so.

Mrs. Ladigan shades her eyes with her hand. "Let's go over to that area." She points. "So we'll have the sea in the background and the sun in front of you." She strides over there and we follow her like baby ducks. She gestures at the water. "There are some sea lions swimming around—maybe grab some footage of that."

We run to the wall to watch the sleek brown forms gliding in and out of the water. "Arf, arf, arf!" Chad imitates their barking. Which they're not actually doing at the moment because they're too busy swimming.

Ryan's dad swings into action, filming them.

"Perfect," Mrs. Ladigan says. "Then get the buskers." She points at the juggler and the other performers.

Miss Gwen's improv team is already here, ten other people standing in the park. They're all ages, from their twenties to their seventies. "Can't wait!" a tall man with a beard says to us. "Is this Ava?"

I nod and shrink behind my dad. Luckily there's some chaos as the grown-ups circle into their team and we circle into ours.

"I'll warm you up," Miss Gwen says. "Zip!" Miss Gwen points at me.

"Zap!" I point at Jonathan.

"Zop!" He points at Cecily.

After the warm-up, Miss Gwen has us huddle together, something I've seen Luke do with his team during soccer games. "What's rule number one of improv?" Miss Gwen makes eye contact with each of us.

"Have fun!" we chorus.

She smiles. "Yes! And remember—support, support, support. Have each other's backs. Ready?" She puts her hand out into the circle. The others put their hands on top of hers. I imitate them, not knowing what's happening. "Count of three. Fosters Freeze Cult."

"One, two, three, FOSTERS FREEZE CULT," they shout.

We watch the grown-up team. They start with an improvised rap, then do some short-form games, like the ones we warm up with. Ryan's dad films them and a crowd gathers around.

Miss Gwen signals us. "Two minutes," she says.

We gather together one more time. "Got your back," Cecily says.

Chad pats me and smiles into my face. "Got your back." It sounds like a promise.

This is what we're doing? I've never told anyone that in my life. It feels awkward, but also good. I pat Jonathan. "Got your back," I say to him, and he grins. And we keep going like that until everyone has said that to each person.

We line up single file. The other team finishes and Miss Gwen steps forward. "And now here we are with our fabulous middle school team, the Fosters Freeze Cult!"

I freeze. Cecily gives me a gentle shove. "You're good, Ava." Then I move forward, finally.

Ryan is going to be the "host," which means he's the one who's going to actually talk to people. "Good afternoon!" Ryan steps forward with his loudest Ryan voice. "We are Fosters Freeze Cult! A group of middle school improvisers here to entertain. Improv means everything we're doing is totally made up on the spot. We will do this show once, and it will never be seen again."

Some people pause to see what we're doing. I realize we're going to have to be extra loud with all the noises around.

It is super weird to have an audience standing so close, not to mention the huge black camera pointed toward us. My arms and legs start tingling as if my body's getting ready to panic. Mr. Matt says sometimes I just have to push through my feeling of being uncomfortable. *Aversion therapy*, he calls it. If you're afraid of spiders, you keep looking at spiders until you're not afraid anymore.

It's hard for me to do when I'm by myself.

Cecily makes eye contact with me and smiles. Now

I don't have to be by myself. If I fall, they'll catch me. They've got my back.

And I've got theirs.

"First I'm going to need your help," Ryan continues. "Could I get a suggestion for the last thing you did at Navegando Point?"

"Rode the carousel!" someone shouts.

"Carousel," we repeat. "Thank you."

Chad steps forward. "The carousel reminds me of the time I spun around so many times I threw up."

"That reminds me of eating too much ice cream," Cecily says. "I only made that mistake once."

"That reminds me of when I was eating ice cream and a seagull took it out of my hand," Chad says.

"That reminds me of when I got lost here when I was little," I say, the memory surfacing. I'd been scared and ended up in the cupcake shop. The owner gave me a mini strawberry cupcake and had me sit down until they found my parents.

"That was scary," Dad says.

That breaks it. "Scary!" we all repeat.

The others walk away and I'm left standing there with Cecily. She's tossing imaginary stuff onto the ground—birdseed, I guess. I decide I'm walking a small dog on a leash. Cecily looks at what I'm doing. "Find any treasure?" she asks in an old lady voice.

I understand that I'm holding a metal detector, not a

dog. I grunt at her. Somehow I'm Luke again. "Just some coins so I can buy a treat." I set down my metal detector. "I'm looking for the cupcake shop. It used to be here."

"Lots of things used to be here," Cecily says. "My husband. My children. My will to live."

"Ooooh," the crowd says.

I sigh. "I have to find it." Suddenly it's the most important thing to this kid, and I remember all over again what it was like to feel so scared, then so happy when I got the mini cupcake. And what it was like to be here with my whole family, when we were all little. There's a new hole now because the cupcake shop is gone.

Nothing will ever be the same.

Cecily's just looking at me, waiting for me to continue.

"I couldn't find any coins." Real tears come to my eyes. "I don't have enough money to buy something else, and now I can't get my parking validated!"

"Oh, sweetie." Cecily holds out her arms to hug me. "I'll validate you."

The crowd laughs. We hug. And the crowd goes quiet, watching me and Cecily have our emotional little moment. Something in the air has changed. I guess it's like watching someone get proposed to or break up in public—everyone has to stop what they're doing and watch.

Just then the developer lady, Brett Rosselin, appears out of an empty restaurant. She marches toward us, her spiky heels leaving holes behind her on the grass.

"What's going on here?" Ryan's dad swings his camera around.

"Shush," a woman in the crowd with a big camera dangling around her neck says. "They're performing."

Brett ignores her. "I know you," Brett says to Nana Linda. "You disrupted our meeting."

Mrs. Ladigan steps forward, her arms crossed. She reminds me of a vice principal. "They're not causing any harm or doing anything illegal."

The woman takes out her phone. "You're not allowed to perform without a permit. I'm calling the police."

"It's not your business to check on us," Nana Linda says.

"Besides which, people are allowed to perform here as long as they don't block the right-of-way. Which they aren't doing. You only need a permit at Balboa Park." Mrs. Ladigan looks ready to throw down with Brett.

A crease appears between Brett's eyebrows. "We are in control of this property now, not you. There are laws."

"The Port of San Diego has jurisdiction, not your development company," Mrs. Ladigan says, her voice all vinegar.

"Just let the kids perform," someone says.

"They're not hurting anything." The juggler comes up next to us.

The balloon lady shakes a bright blue balloon sword. "Let them be free!"

Brett turns from everyone and takes a step away.

"Hello? Yes," she says into her phone. "This is an emergency. There's a crowd—a gang—of teenagers here damaging my property and being disorderly."

What? I hope the microphone catches her. This is just an outright lie. First of all, I'm not even a teenager. Second, if we're damaging property, then everyone in this park is, too.

"You're being ridiculous." Mrs. Ladigan's face reddens. Brett ignores her, talking to the police.

My stomach goes hot as I get an idea. Either a no-good, awful, terrible idea, or the last one I ever have because it will kill me dead.

It's the kind of thing Zelia would do, actually, if she were here. But she's not and I am. Maybe I'll be better, maybe worse.

Only one way to find out.

I step forward and take in a deep breath. Get ready because Ava Andrews is going to talk. "But you're the one hurting everything." I point at her as dramatically as I can. "She's going to tear down Navegando Point!"

She rolls her eyes. "Not me personally."

"They're going to put up a high-rise hotel," I inform the crowd.

"They raised the rent so most of the shops have closed," Cecily says.

"That's because they can't compete," Brett says sharply.

Chad steps forward and sinks dramatically to his

knees. "No more cupcakes!" he wails.

"No more parking!" Ryan shouts.

"No more family time," Cecily yells.

"No balloon animals or jugglers," Babel declares.

"This will all be gone!" Chad says dramatically.

"You'll have nothing left but a hideous pile of concrete that will burn your eyes," Jonathan informs them.

We make eye contact with each other. Then I say—

And this is kind of the miraculous part—

We all say it together.

"Rescue Navegando Point now!" we yell.

And we start spinning like we've practiced it, but we haven't.

The woman blinks.

The crowd cheers.

The juggler starts throwing pins into the air.

Ryan's dad captures it all.

Two cops on bicycles ride up the sidewalk. Their uniforms are shorts and short-sleeves, and handcuffs dangle from their belts. I swallow nervously. Brett Rosselin waves them over. "Here."

"Where?" One gets off her bike. "We got a report of vandalism and disorderly conduct?"

"Here!" Brett points at us.

The police officers look at us. "You called 911 for this?" the other cop asks, shaking his head.

"Well, they stopped." Brett tosses her head.

Ryan's dad steps forward, swinging his camera off his

shoulder. "Interesting. Because I have it all recorded, if you want to watch the footage."

"And we never did one illegal thing," Mrs. Ladigan points out.

The police officers lean over his shoulders as they review the show. They smile a couple times.

"You guys didn't come up with that ahead of time?" one of them says. "Amazing."

"I was thinking of taking a class," the man says.

"You totally should," Miss Gwen says. "We have a free introductory one. I'll get you the info."

"Enough!" Brett's practically turned into a beet. "Are you going to cite them or aren't you?"

"No. But we might cite *you* for wasting police resources," the female officer says. She waves at us. "You kids can go."

Brett sticks her phone back into her purse. "I'm only doing my job."

The officers look at her like my mom looked at me when I said I didn't eat the entire package of Oreos even though I had crumbs all over my face.

Mrs. Ladigan cocks an eyebrow at the developer. "I'd say you're doing it rather poorly."

Chad holds an invisible bottle up to Brett. "Want some aloe for that burn?" We can't help it. We giggle. I decide I like Mrs. Ladigan. She's salty and she's fearless.

Miss Gwen gestures at us to move. "Let's get going while the going's good."

We trot away. "Keep fighting, kids!" someone calls.

"Good luck!" someone else adds.

Mrs. Ladigan's redness finally fades. "If I wasn't committed to you before, I am now. I am fired up!"

"You'd better watch out when my mom gets fired up about something," Becca says.

Mrs. Ladigan points a finger at the sky. "They are going to rue the day! That footage is great."

"Yes!" Nana Linda gives her a high five. "I love making people rue the day."

"She's going to rue ever being born!" Chad yells. "Her descendants will disown her! The ghosts of her ancestors will haunt her forever for being mean!"

"Calm down, dude." Cecily gives him a friendly shove.

But it might be Ryan's dad who's the most excited. "Yes!" He lopes around us, exactly like a bigger version of Ryan. "Awesome job, everyone! Simply awesome."

Ryan sticks his arms out like an airplane and zooms between us. Then we all do it and people are getting out of our way and also looking at us as though we've lost our minds. But I don't care.

Not one bit.

CHAPTER 32

After school on Monday, I'm walking out when I see Mr. Sukow standing with Ms. Bookstein in the courtyard. "Ava!" he says. "Great video."

"Really good stuff." Ms. Bookstein thumbs-ups me.

My heart does a double beat and my back goes warm. "You saw it?"

"The teachers shared it." Mr. Sukow looks at me as if I've just won the Nobel Prize for Videos. "You really spoke up, Ava. I'm so impressed. They're naming the woman who called the police Protest Patty."

"Her name is Brett," I say, not understanding.

"It's a joke," Mr. Sukow explains. "A nickname. People are upset that someone did that to kids."

"The Rescue Navegando Point Now! page shared it." Ms. Bookstein whips out her phone and shows me. "Ten thousand views so far!"

"Ten thousand?" I squeak. I sit down on a bench.

Ten thousand people have seen me?

Cecily and Ryan and Chad all sort of show up at the same time. "Did you hear? Ten thousand views!" Ryan whoops. "Insane!"

"I heard," I say faintly. I put my hand on my pacemaker. My heart's beating a little hard, but I'm okay.

"You're going to the next community meeting, aren't you?" Mr. Sukow sits next to me. "You should really capitalize on the video."

"How?" A little flutter goes through me, not nervousness, exactly. More like I'm about to put the last piece in a jigsaw puzzle.

"Make a new Facebook page. Organize." Ms. Bookstein sits on my other side.

"How?" I repeat. "I'm not allowed to have any social media."

"I can help, if you want," Mr. Sukow says. "I used to do some community organizing back in the day."

"I'll share the online petition with the PTA and all my librarian groups," Ms. Bookstein adds.

All us kids look at each other. They nod. I nod. "We're in."

Ms. Bookstein makes a Facebook page for us. She puts the video on there, front and center. "I'll ask the other page to link to us, so we can join forces," she says, "but still be separate."

259

"Sounds good," I say. "The San Diego historical land-mark committee never emailed Nana Linda back."

Ms. Bookstein sighs. "Typical bureaucracy. Maybe they'll respond next year. Now let's make an event invitation." She brings up that page. "Your turn."

I pause. "What should it say?"

"Let's take over the Port of San Diego!" Chad says.

"Bring your torches and pitchforks!" Ryan says.

"Um, no," Cecily says.

"How about this?" I type:

Your one and only chance to keep making memories with your family.
Navegando Point is a big part of a lot of San Diegans' memories. A place to spend time with your family by the water. But that's all going to change.
The question is, do you want it to?

"Great." Ms. Bookstein posts it.

I'm a little sick to my stomach again. Now even more people are going to read my writing. What if internet trolls make mean comments?

I clench my jaw. "I don't care what other people think," I say out loud. "I can't control them."

Ms. Bookstein blinks. "That's true, Ava."

"Fist bump." Cecily holds out her knuckles to me.

We tap. Cecily twirls around in her chair. "Can we get T-shirts?"

Mr. Sukow nods. "That would be an excellent idea."

And just like that, I'm a rabble-rousing activist.

Nana Linda's going to be very proud.

CHAPTER 33

The next afternoon, Ty and I stand in the hallway outside the English classroom, getting our napkin presentation ready to go.

My stomach jumps around. Ty looks more nervous than I am, actually—he's wearing a light pink dress shirt and he's sweated through the armpits. "Did I tell you that my mom shared the video with a bunch of people?"

"Nope." I blush. "I didn't even know you watched it!"

"You were great." Ty looks sideways at me. "Really."

"Thanks," I mutter. I still feel shy about accepting compliments.

"She's going to the protest—all the business owners are." He shrugs. "Maybe it'll help. She really liked working there—she was assistant manager. I liked it because she got free cupcakes."

I giggle.

He bends over, his hand on his stomach. "Ooof. I feel like I'm going to barf. How do you do improv?"

I take stock of myself. No throw-up feeling. No frozen one. Nervous, yes. "I guess doing it with people I like helps."

"Hmm," he grumps.

I think about Ryan again, and his former bullying days. "Ty, maybe you could go to improv, too." But what if his mom can't afford it? They must have scholarships or something. I don't know.

"It sounds scary."

"It is at first. But then it's not. And the kids are really cool." I look at Ty's nervous face and think about him eating lunch alone. He needs to be included, too. I make an offer. "We're trick-or-treating together in my neighborhood—you could come."

His eyes get big and his mouth opens. "Um . . . I don't know."

"You can think about it." I didn't mean to put him on the spot right before our presentation.

Mr. Sukow pokes his head out. "Come on in."

I hold up my fist for him to bump. "This is going to be the best napkin presentation in the history of napkins."

We didn't try to rewrite the lost script. Instead, we came up with a whole new one, and we talked it out like we were in improv together.

Ty returns the bump. "Darn straight it is."

The Napkin That Saved the World

Ty: Once upon a time, there was a supervillain named Jerome. He was eating a club sandwich, packed with juicy tomatoes and too much mayo.

Ava: Once upon a time, there was a supervillain named Millicent, who was eating a dripping soft-serve cone.

Ty: They both wanted one thing.

Ava: To rule the world.

Ty: As soon as they finished lunch.

(They bite into their meals.)

Ava: Ugh, this ice cream is dripping down my arm!

Ty: Argh, this tomato juice got on my shirt!

(They both reach for the only napkin and hold it up in between them.)

Ava (in a villainous voice): Jerome.

Ty (in an even more villainous voice):
Millicent.

Ava: We meet again.

Ty: Indeed. I trust your plans for world
domination are not coming along well.

Ava: On the contrary, they're much better
than yours.

(They wrestle with the napkin.)

Ava: I need that!

Ty: Not more than I need it!

(The napkin tears in half.)

Ava: Look what you did.

Ty: You should have let go.

Ava: I will never let go.

(They each dab at themselves with their
half of the napkin.)

Ty: Interesting. Half the napkin was enough for my needs!

Ava: Even more interesting. Half the napkin took care of this ice-cream mess!

(Ava and Ty look at each other.)

Ava: I suppose we could share.

Ty: That reminds me. I found a way to harness the power of the sun to fuel my robot army.

Ava: How wonderful! And that reminds me. I found a way to use a robot army to take over the moon.

Ty: How wonderful.

Ava: Are you thinking what I'm thinking?

Ty: That I should have gotten a lemonade?

Ava: That everyone should buy this napkin!

(Ty offers his hand to Ava. They shake.)

Ava: I think this is the beginning of a
beautiful friendship.

"Scene!" I yell.

And then Ty actually grabs my hand and we bow deep, from the waist. I hear the kids clapping but it really doesn't matter.

We did it.

"Woo-hoo, Ava!" Cecily yells.

I scurry to my desk and collapse onto my folded arms.

CHAPTER 34

"Do you have the candy map?" asks Jonathan. His cowboy boots clack on the sidewalk. He's dressed as Woody from *Toy Story* and his costume's so realistic that he looks more like he belongs at Comic-Con than trick-or-treating.

"We don't need a candy map," Ryan says, his voice muffled. He's dressed as a T. rex in an oversized, puffy costume. I hope he can see. "We'll just knock."

They're talking about the Nextdoor app—it has a virtual map where people can put a pin by their house if they're giving out candy. Green pins mean they've got allergy-friendly stuff, too. "A lot of people don't add their houses to the app. My parents didn't," I tell them.

Speaking of whom, my parents are standing on the front porch. "Be sure to say thank you!" Dad calls.

"And be considerate of smaller kids," Mom adds.

"And no pranks," Dad says. I'm pretty sure he's

directing that at Ryan and Chad.

"Me? I would never consider such a thing." Chad shakes his head. He's got a surfer outfit on, board shorts and a Hawaiian shirt, with thick white sunblock smeared over his nose. Or maybe he's a tourist. It doesn't really matter.

"Don't worry." Cecily salutes my father. "I've got the situation handled."

Ty, in his pirate costume, trips on a crack, and Chad catches him by the elbow. "Arrr, matey, you've got to be more careful!"

"Aye, aye, Captain!" Ty straightens and smiles at me. I smile back. I wasn't worried that anyone secretly didn't want Ty to join. He came along and became part of us. No big deal.

We walk as one group, like a school of fish, down the sidewalk. In each of our buckets is an idea Mrs. Ladigan came up with. We've got slips of paper to hand out to the houses, with our Facebook page address on them. We're going to give one to every grown-up we see. Every little bit helps.

I turn and look back at my house. My parents are still there, waving. "Are they going to stand there all night?" I ask. It's my first time trick-or-treating without them, and I want to dance around and sing, but not while they're watching.

"They'll go back in once you're out of sight," Cecily

says confidently. She's a vampire, with a wig and white makeup and fangs that she's glued onto her real teeth. "That's what parents do. Don't worry."

"I'm not. Not really." I adjust my robe. I'm Ruth Vader Ginsburg, which was pretty easy to do. My mom found me a lace collar like the one the judge wears to the Supreme Court, and loaned me her best Darth Vader helmet. She saw a costume like it on the internet and, after she laughed hysterically for about ten minutes, convinced me to wear it.

Ryan stops at a driveway two houses down. Their jack-o'-lantern is lit and the porch light is on. "This one!" He scampers up the driveway as if he's a five-year-old all over again.

Cecily grabs my hand. "Come on!" And then I feel like a five-year-old, too, giggling and skipping with my friend. Like I imagined when we first met.

My phone buzzes, and I drop Cecily's hand and pause on the walkway to the front door. I lift my robe to take it out of my jeans pocket. It's not my parents, but Zelia.

I stand there with the phone for a minute, considering. I haven't talked to her since before my pacemaker thing, since the day she told me she didn't want me to come. We'd just messaged and of course she'd told me to feel better and all that. But I haven't responded.

The front door of the house opens, and a lady in a witch's hat passes out full-sized candy bars. My friends scream.

My friends. Plural. Unbelievable. I've never been so comfortable with a group of people other than my family. Or felt so accepted.

Like I belong.

"Where's Ava?" Ryan asks, turning, almost knocking over a potted plant with his tail.

I take a deep breath and hit the red button on the phone. I'll call Zelia back later. "I'm right here."

CHAPTER 35

Halloween was a success. Mom says I scored enough candy for the rest of my childhood, so I donate half of it to a military group. Maybe more important, though, is we leave those slips of paper about the protest with people.

Ryan, of course, talked to each house, and the rest of us acted so goofy in our characters that people wanted to know about improv and Navegando Point. And over the next week, the hits on the Facebook page and the video keep going up. We're at five hundred thousand views. There are thousands of signatures. It's pretty awesome.

Now I'm in the living room, watching the news with my parents. It's the night before the protest where we're all going to meet at the Port of San Diego for the hearing.

Luke comes out of his room. "Mom, I need help with math."

Mom rubs her hands together. "Oh boy! Have a seat, my son."

Luke groans. "Promise me you won't call the teacher."

"I can make no promises," Mom says.

Luke shakes his head at me. "Ava, where did we get these parents?"

I shrug, grinning. Ever since Luke and I had our "Hallmark card moment," as he calls it, we've been getting along much better. It's like my heart thing made the tension between us burst.

"Ava!" Mom turns up the volume. "You're on!" She points at the screen.

"And in local news," the news anchor lady with the fluffy blond hair is saying, "some local middle schoolers got in a scuffle with a real estate developer over Navegando Point. Just watch."

They show a clip of us performing. I blanch, knowing what's coming. Me. I want to cover my eyes, but I don't. I watch myself and Cecily perform, expecting we're terrible, but we're actually not. You can tell both of us are having fun. Maybe if you have fun, you can't be terrible. "I was walking a dog but Cecily said I was using a metal detector," I say to Mom and Dad.

"And you switched right away—good job having her back," Mom says.

"You see? There's no such thing as failure in improv," Dad says, and I can tell he's warming up to a lecture.

Then Ryan's dad zooms in as Brett breaks her way into our group.

And then there I am, pointing at her. I actually look pretty dramatic.

I put my face in my hands as the police get there. It looks so bad for Brett that I almost feel sorry for her. Almost. "Oh my gosh," I breathe.

"If you want to be part of the community redevelopment hearing with these kids, their Facebook page is here." The address flashes up on the screen. "There will be a protest tomorrow."

I let out a muffled little shriek.

"This is amazing, Ava!" Dad high-fives me.

"That's going to get you so many views!" Mom declares.

I grab my phone and group text.

I never thought I'd say this, but I can't wait to go to a boring grown-up meeting! I write, and wait as the responses come rolling in.

Then it hits me—it didn't even occur to me to text Zelia.

Does this mean we're not friends anymore at all?

It's as if my insides have been put into a blender. I sink low into the sofa and pull my T-shirt up to my eyeballs, over my mouth and nose, breathing in and out hard. Trying to control my emotions.

"What's wrong?" Luke surprises me by saying. Like he's actually paying attention to my mood.

I sigh. Mom mutes the news and all of them are looking at me. I might as well tell them what's going on. "I'm
having a problem." I tell them the whole thing.

"Well, do you want to go out there?" Dad says. "And
did you tell her?"

"Wait a minute." Mom holds up her hand. "Ava, do
you want us to offer suggestions, or do you just want to
talk?"

I think about it for a minute. "I guess suggestions
would be good. And yes, Dad, I told her I wanted to."

"There must be more to the story than Zelia's told you."
Mom taps her pencil. "That sounds very unlike her."

"Why wouldn't she just tell me?" I ask.

"Maybe Maine made her weird." Luke blows eraser
dust off his paper. "Maybe Maine turned her into you."

"Gee, thanks," I say. But Luke might be onto something there. Like being new made Zelia shy, or something.
That's something to think about.

"Call her and hash it out." Dad unmutes the news as
sports comes on. "That's the only way to solve the problem. You two have been friends for too long to let this
come between you."

I turn my phone over in my hands. I guess they're
right. Maybe.

I go into my room and FaceTime Zelia. She answers.
"Hey, Ava!" She speaks like we just talked to each other
five minutes ago, not before Halloween. An entire month

ago. "Is everything all right?" She chews on her lip. "I know you were mad the last time we talked." Zelia puts a hand over her heart. "This okay?"

"It's fine." I shoot her a quick smile. I need to get this out before I lose courage. "I wanted to talk to you about the visit."

She blinks. "What about it?"

I purse my lips. "I want to go out there. I told you."

She blinks again, hard, in the dramatic way she has when she *wants* me to notice her blinking. That means she's getting mad. I don't usually protest when Zelia tells me stuff. She's in charge.

This isn't always a good thing. To have one person always be the boss and the other person do what they say, even if that other person has her own opinions and thoughts.

And then I decide it doesn't matter if Zelia gets upset. I have to be honest. There's no other way. I pull my shoulder blades together like I'm a brave kind of character. "Zelia, you're not the only one who gets to decide stuff."

She blinks again, softer this time. "I know."

"You told me to tell you when I wanted something. And I did. And you acted like what I think doesn't matter." My voice rises. "I want to know why."

She opens her mouth to deny this, probably, but then seems to have a thought and closes it. She moves her shoulders and lets her hair hang in front of her face. "It's just that . . ." Zelia sighs. "I really kind of hate it here."

What? "I thought you liked it. The leaves and the theater and your new friends."

"I know I should, I know I should be happy that my mom's got a full-time job she likes and everything. But it's hard to make friends when you're new and they've all known each other since kindergarten." Zelia starts sniffling. "And they all go on fancy vacations and they talk down about improv."

I go quiet. I can't imagine having to deal with all that. Some of it, sure. But not all of it at the same time. "I'm sorry. That must be hard. But what does that have to do with me visiting? Doesn't that make you want me to come out there?"

"Well, finding out how *you're* making friends, and doing improv like I used to . . ." Zelia closes her eyes as if she's in pain. "I don't want to say it."

"Say it." I shake my head. "I won't be mad." I mean it. She could tell me she was plotting a nefarious crime against me right now and I would not be angry at her. I know what's going on with me now, from the story. Now I just want to know what's going on with *her*.

"Promise?"

"I promise," I say.

Her breath catches. "I'm jealous."

Jealous? Of me?

That's impossible.

I actually get a little mad in spite of myself. She should be happy for me. I was the one left behind. What was I supposed to do? Eat lunch alone forever? Never make another friend? I was *alone*.

Be vulnerable, I hear Miss Gwen say. *Sit in the moment*.

"Ava?" Zelia says worriedly. "It's just that you're out there living your best life and I'm here and all depressed and it's just too hard. I was thinking it'd be better if we didn't even talk anymore, you know?" She rubs her eyes. "I miss you too much. Are you mad? I'm gross and terrible, I know. You should be mad. I was awful."

I shake my head. I breathe in, figuring out what I'm feeling. "I'm not mad. Well, a little." Zelia is jealous of me. This is not something I thought would happen, ever. But I think about it from her point of view. Her having to wear itchy woolen sweaters and trying to make new friends with kids that maybe aren't as friendly as the improv kids. That feeling of watching someone else live the life you wish you could have, while you watch, stuck in place.

And all at once I know exactly what she's talking about. I know because that's how it used to be for me. All the time.

I would never want that for her.

The anger fades out as quickly as it showed up. Instead, a warmth spreads through me. I smile at her.

She smiles back at me, waiting. One breath, then two.

Finally I say the truest thing that's in my heart. "I wish you were here so I could give you a big fat hug."

Her eyes flash upward, meet mine. "Really? I've hated myself for feeling that petty. It's so gross." Zelia sniffles. "The only way I could deal with it was by not talking to you so much. And not seeing you this summer."

This reminds me of something, sort of. Once, Hudson had a huge crush on one of his friends who didn't like him back that way. When she stopped coming over, I asked him what happened. He said not seeing her at all was easier.

"Were you . . ." I squint, figuring this out. "Trying to protect yourself?" So that's why she's been like that. It explains everything. I nod. "I get it. But I wish . . ." I shake my head. "I want us both to be happy."

"I am happy for you," she says. "I'm just not happy for me."

I reach my hand into the air, toward the camera. She reaches out hers. We squeeze the air and, as we make eye contact, I pretend I'm sending my energy through the phone, into the satellite in space, and then bouncing it back down to the other side of the country.

I swear, just for a second, there's warmth and pressure. For the first time in a long time I feel connected to her.

My best friend.

CHAPTER 36

On the day of the protest, Nana Linda drives me down to the Port of San Diego offices. I'm so queasy I almost barfed this morning, but Dad made me eat some toast, and then I practiced my deep breathing, so I'm feeling sort of okay. Almost.

Mr. Sukow and Ms. Bookstein are already in front, with big cardboard boxes of bright green T-shirts that say *Rescue Navegando Point Now!* on them. Mrs. Ladigan suggested we get them to make us look unified. "Looks like it's going well!" Nana Linda takes shirts for us.

I look around. There are like a hundred people here, so many I can't even count.

"Hi." Mrs. Ladigan's touching my arm. She's wearing a bright red blazer with matching lipstick. It looks like battle armor to me. "You ready?"

I shrug, swallowing down the nerves. "No. I mean

yes. I mean, I don't know."

"I'll get in there first. I'm the facts. You guys are the emotion." She winks at me. "You got this."

"Ava!" Ty's shouting at me. He walks over with his mom, and a woman with oversized glasses I don't recognize.

The woman in the glasses says, "You were so great in the video!"

I feel myself flush. "Um, thanks?"

"You're welcome!" She cocks her head at me. "You don't remember me, do you?"

I squint at her and shake my head. "I don't."

"This is the cupcake shop owner, Laura Camacho," Ty's mother says.

Ms. Camacho points to her curly hair. "Usually my cap flattens this out."

"Oh!" Now I remember her, kind of. "I'm sorry your shop got closed."

She nods, her mouth set in a firm line. "I'm hoping the Port of San Diego will restore the rents to what they used to be. Then we can reopen." She sighs. "You did something to get people out here. No matter what happens, that is huge." She offers me her hand, and I shake it. Nice and firm.

"We'll see you in there, Ava." Ty's mom waves.

Ty gives me a thumbs-up. I return it. Never in a million years did I think that I would be friends with Ty.

Really, it all came down to us listening to and understanding each other's point of view. Without that, we'd still be enemies.

I take in a deep breath and look around. I can't spot Nana Linda and my teachers in the sea of green, but that's okay. I'm not lost. Still, my body's shaking a little, as if it can't let go of all the anxiety.

I hop up and down, moving the energy through me.

Miss Gwen appears next to me. "Ava!" She gives me a hug. "So proud of you, girl."

"Thank you." I squeeze her back. Miss Gwen's opinion matters a lot. I've never had a coach before, so I never understood why Luke looked up to his soccer coaches or why Hudson always talks about his dance instructors.

"Come on. The group's over here." She nods at me. "You ready?"

"As ready as I'll ever be." Everything on my body is quivering.

"You'll do great."

I spot my improv group standing in a circle—Ryan's reddish hair is always a dead giveaway. "Hey," I say. They part to let me into the group.

"What's up, crazy pup?" Ryan high-fives me.

My pulse starts to speed up, thinking of going into the meeting with all these people. "I'm just trying not to die from nerves."

They all look at me seriously. I shake my head. "I'm joking."

Cecily claps me on the back. "Too soon, Ava. Too soon."

We file into the small auditorium and walk down to the first row. Some tables are set up in front of the audience, and the Port of San Diego people sit there, with paper name plates propped up, and microphones on stands. There are about fifteen of them. I see Brett Rosselin standing at the podium, talking to a man in a suit. She turns as our footsteps echo through the hall.

The color drains from her face. Good. *Be afraid,* I want to tell Brett. *We are here and we will not be quiet!*

Uh-oh. I'm turning into Nana Linda. I giggle to myself.

The man in the suit puts his hand over the mic, but we're close enough for me to hear him ask, "What's all this?"

"I . . . I don't know," Brett stammers. She leans into the mic. "Excuse me, are you all here for the Navegando Point meeting?"

"Can't you read, lady?" A woman points to her shirt.

Brett blinks. "Of course I can read. But I would behoove you to sit down."

"Is that even the right way to use *behoove*?" Cecily whispers.

"I don't think so," I whisper back.

Miss Gwen signs up on the speaker list. I look to see what it says. Each person gets two minutes.

Nana Linda signs up. And Mr. Sukow. And Ms. Bookstein.

That's eight minutes for us.

I blow out a breath.

Cecily takes my hand. Hers is kind of sweaty. "You okay?"

"I'm okay. You okay?" On my other side, I squeeze Ryan's hand.

"I'm okay. *You* okay?" Ryan responds.

On his other side, Chad says, "*I'm* okay; you're okay."

"I'm okay, and *you* are also very okay," Babel says.

"We're all okay," Jonathan ends.

Brett is staring at us as if we're in here planning to graffiti the place instead of talk. "If you try anything, you will be asked to leave."

"Excuse me?" Miss Gwen stands up. "Please do not try to discipline my well-behaved students."

Brett makes a weird little spitting noise, like a mad cat. She turns back to the podium. "Let us call this meeting to order."

The man in the suit does a slide show about the proposal. "As you know, Navegando Point is a derelict collection of overpriced shops whose business has been declining for decades. We at the Brancusi Group seek a new vision, one that will make San Diego a world-class destination."

What are they talking about? San Diego's already a world-class destination. But we listen intently. The plan is to take our inspiration from whatever this speech is about.

"As such, we will have a five-star hotel plus a boutique hotel where the park now is, with luxury stores along the bottom facing the water. A walkway along the water will remain. The hotels will bring much-needed rooms to San Diego." He points. "Additionally, there will be an aquarium for scientific study and education." He directs a smile toward us, like he thinks we'll fall for it.

I try not to think about what's coming next—us. Or what's at stake—just the theater. The cupcake shop. Real estate prices. Basically everything.

No big deal.

Brett puts her finger on the speech list. "We will now take comments from the public. You each have two minutes." She looks down. "Sheila Ladigan."

Mrs. Ladigan pops up from a few rows back. She gives me a little wave and I wave back. Then she strides up there like she owns the whole place. I straighten up in my chair. I'll be like her, I decide. Channel Mrs. Ladigan.

She stands at the podium with a confident smile.

"You have in front of you a packet containing a petition, alternate blueprints, and more."

The Port Authority people shuffle around. I crane my neck. Yup, each of them has a stapled report or something. Mrs. Ladigan sure is on top of things.

She holds up a piece of paper and swivels so we can see it, too. It's a printout of the final tally for our online signatures. "Twenty thousand people signed this petition. Twenty thousand devoted to saving Navegando Point." She shakes her head. "What I'd like to know is why the Port of San Diego has not considered the alternate plan to leave the historical area alone and continue redeveloping the other part."

"We have considered it," Brett says, her voice unwavering. "It's not feasible."

"In what way is it not feasible?" Mrs. Ladigan holds up a report folder. "I ran the numbers. In terms of cost-benefit, it works out better. In terms of environmental impact, it works out *much* better." She leans on the podium and stares intently at the committee. It's like she's sending her enthusiasm at them through her eyeballs. It's pretty exciting to watch. I wonder how much of this confidence she learned from Cotillion. "And in terms of what the community wants, it is the only way."

Everyone claps. Brett stands. "That's time." She looks at the clipboard, not commenting anymore on what Mrs. Ladigan says. Mrs. Ladigan takes a seat near us in the front. "Gwen Vercoe, you're up."

"I give my two minutes to these students," Miss Gwen says.

Brett shakes her head and purses her lips. "I'm so sorry. That's not how we do it." She points to the next name. "Linda Kingston?"

"I do the same," Nana Linda calls.

"As do I," Ms. Bookstein says.

"And I." Mr. Sukow stands. "There's nothing in your rules that state we can't do this."

"But they're children," Brett says.

Ms. Camacho steps forward. "We want to hear from them!"

"Yeah," the rest of the crowd choruses.

One of the Port of San Diego people gestures Brett over. They have a whispered conference. Then Brett turns around. "Proceed," she barks.

We stand up. I get a weird sensation like I'm floating above my body, as if I'm not really here at all.

Cecily grips my hand. And just like that, I'm anchored.

She and I step out, still holding hands. I take a breath and catch Mrs. Ladigan's eye. She nods and gives me a thumbs-up.

I'm going to be like her. Act like her, at least. I'm going to take my energy and send it out. I shake out my sweaty hands.

We take turns reading our new letters, as we planned.

"Navegando Point is where I first saw jugglers and performers and thought, *I want to do that*." Ryan reads first. He continues about having family picnics by the water.

Cecily goes next. "I didn't start going there until improv, and then we went every weekend. We stayed for lunch every Saturday."

I swallow. I wish I wasn't going last. My mouth goes dry.

Babel. "We always take our visiting family to Navegando Point. It's a place that's special to us."

I feel sick to my stomach again. I hop up and down a tiny bit to distract myself.

Chad. "I've never had ice cream or gyros as good as the ones here. If nothing else, you should keep the improv place and these restaurants and maybe open more arts stuff."

I watch the audience reactions. During different parts, they look interested. Or bored.

As the others read, the bubbles in my stomach feel like a shaken-up soda can. I hope I don't burst and run out of here.

"Ava." Miss Gwen's smiling gently at me. "Ready?"

I stand up, my knees shaking. The bubbles are like an engine now, pushing me forward. Helping. "When I was little, I got lost at Navegando Point," I read out loud into the mic, my voice trembling only a little. "I turned around and I couldn't find my family. I was panicked and alone. I started crying, and some man tried to help me, but I got scared and started running. I ran straight into the cupcake shop.

"The owner saw me right away and came out from behind the counter. She hugged me and gave me a cupcake and told me I was going to be fine. She recognized me, but she didn't know where my parents were. She called all the shop owners looking for my parents, telling them to find them and let them know I was in the cupcake shop. Then she let me watch her make cupcakes while I waited. It was the only thing that calmed me down. She treated me like her own kid."

The audience goes quiet, like they're really listening. This is what I have as my weapon—my words. I steal a glance at Brett. She's looking at her fingernails.

"And that is why gentrification is bad. We don't need more luxury shopping outlets. We need places that build community. Where families like mine can enjoy the natural beauty of San Diego while not paying too much money. That is what this city needs most of all." I look up at the Port of San Diego board. Most of them are smiling. I think they look impressed because, hey, I'm only eleven, and I think I did a good job. Like a fifty-year-old attorney, practically. "Thank you."

The audience erupts into applause. I look out at them and for the first time notice a news camera. I swallow hard. Again? The reporter from the news waves at me. I wave back, and so does the rest of my team.

The Port of San Diego board members motion the Brancusi Group people over to them, and they huddle in a tight circle.

"No!" Brett says loudly.

"Come on," I mutter. I stand taller, my hands clenching into fists. As if I could fight all of them single-handedly, though what I can do is maybe raise my voice a little bit.

"We don't exactly have a choice," the head of the Port of San Diego, an older white man, says.

The news lady comes over to me, interrupting my eavesdropping. I wish she would go sit down. "Ava Andrews, the little girl who stood up to the developers. It's a real David versus Goliath story."

The camera person is behind her, recorder on. I can tell because there's a red light like on Ryan's dad's camera.

I'm totally caught off-guard. Why is she talking to *me*? I stare into the camera, my eyes feeling as big as two moons, my mouth open. "Uhhhhhhhh." I freeze, the red light on top hypnotizing me. I can't even think of what to say. "Umm," I try again. Great, Ava. Just great.

"She's the girl." Cecily saves me, sticking her face in front of mine, her arm around me. "But aren't you supposed to get her parents' permission before you interview her?"

Now it's the news lady's turn to say "Um."

A security guard appears out of nowhere, ushering the news people back to their spot. "Please interview afterward, ma'am."

"Attention!" The head of the Port of San Diego clears his throat. "Take your seats."

"Where should we take them?" Ryan whispers, and I giggle, though I can't believe he would make such a terrible Dad joke at a time like this. We all flop back into our chairs. What's going to happen now? I look at Brett Rosselin. She's chewing on her well-manicured hot-pink fingernail.

I sit up straight.

The older Port of San Diego man speaks into his microphone. "I think the children and Mrs. Ladigan make some good points." He glances nervously at the video camera. I bet they never had a news team in here before.

"Yes," another board member chimes in. "And there's obviously a lot of community support for keeping the old part of Navegando Point. Twenty thousand people signed the petition."

The crowd applauds.

"I propose a vote," yet another board member says. "To take a look at the plan to exclude the four-point-five acres of old Navegando Point from being developed."

"This is already a settled matter," Brett says.

"Nothing is settled until it's actually done," the board member says.

I hold my breath.

"Aye!" the board members exclaim. All their hands go up.

My fingers clench the sides of my seat. Could it be . . . ?

"All opposed?" The older dude looks around.

Crickets.

He taps a gavel on the table. "Motion carried."

"Yesssss!" we yell, and Ryan hops up from his seat into the air.

"Shhh," some adult says.

"Take it outside," Brett barks, which I hope are her final words to us forever.

Ryan leads us out of the room, through the dim lobby, pushing through the double doors into the bright squinty sunshine, and it feels like we're escaping a cave. "Woo!" Chad does a cartwheel on the lawn.

"Our show shall go on!" Ryan raises his fist to the sky as if he's King Arthur. "Lo, though ye tried to slay us, ye evil developers, ye must bow. Bow to the power of our child army!" He points a pretend sword at Chad, who falls to the ground.

I laugh. "Yes!" I clap. It worked! Everything we did actually changed someone's mind. Of course, it took a whole lot of people. "We won!" I say, kind of disbelievingly. "We really won." The shops will stay open. I can keep going there with my family. With my friends.

"Darn straight we did!" Cecily hugs me, and then the others join in, and we're a jumble of hugs and limbs and warmth and a little bit stinky, like puppies in a pile, and it's this feeling that I like best of all. I'm part of this pack, this team.

I belong.

I'm so glad I listened to Nana Linda for once.

CHAPTER 37

It's the final Cotillion of the year, held the first week of December. Mom comes with us. Today we're having a showcase, where the kids show the parents what we've learned, and the parents dance with the kids. Mom wants to see how I'm doing even though she's, you know, married to the dude who runs the whole thing, and she knows exactly what I've learned already. I think that makes Mom a super-committed parent. I'm not sure I would do that if I were in her place. Probably, if I were a grown-up, I'd tell my husband I wanted to stay at home with a book and my kid could show me their manners in my own living room.

Tonight I should feel extra nervous with Mom's eagle eyes watching me from the audience, her phone raised to capture all kinds of embarrassing video and photos. And I do have a few butterflies, but it's more like I'm also excited.

Sort of like I am during improv.

Mom flashes a thumbs-up at me and I roll my eyes dramatically, but I don't really mean it. She'll film me and take photos, especially when I have to do the parent-child dance with Dad, but somehow I'll be okay. Both my brothers were.

"Everyone line up. Boys over here, girls over there. The first dance will be the foxtrot." Dad starts the music, but it's not Frank Sinatra for once. It's a modern song, "Ho Hey," by the Lumineers. I catch his eye and he winks. He finally listened.

The boys start walking across the room. By now they're used to doing this. So am I. For a second I want to hang back, like usual, but instead I find my feet moving and decide to follow them instead, right into the center of the boys.

They part around me like I'm a tree in a river, none of them looking at me. In the past this would make me feel rejected, but I'm not worried. I'll find someone to dance with.

Someone grabs my hand from the side, and I pull it away and whirl to face him. "You're supposed to make eye contact and ask before you touch me," I inform him.

It's Ryan. His face turns the same shade as his hair.

"It's you!" I point at him. I couldn't have been more surprised if one of my brothers had shown up. Then I remember his mom saying she needed to enroll him. I give him a playful tap on the shoulder. "Way to start the class late—just in time for the party."

"That's my style." He grins, the flush fading.

I smile back, and hold out my hands. "Ask me."

He glances around, listens to what the other boys are saying, then bows from the waist. "Would you care to dance, mademoiselle?" he says in a French accent.

"Oui." I giggle.

"Like this?" He puts his right hand on my waist, puts his left in my right.

"Yup. But you're not supposed to pick a dance partner on purpose." I drop my accent.

He crosses his heart and drops his accent, too. "I swear to you on my Dungeon Master's guide, I did not try to choose you. Until I saw you." Ryan laughs. "Anyway, what are you, a Pokémon? Also, why do the boys choose the girls? Is this 1980?"

I giggle. "Dad wishes."

Ryan looks down at his feet. "How do I . . . ?"

"Step forward with your left foot, then your right. We're basically going to draw a square," I tell him, and even though I'm not supposed to lead, I sort of do, moving my right foot back and dragging him along.

"Small talk," Dad intones in his microphone.

Ryan whispers, "Is this small enough?"

"Even smaller." I lower my voice even more.

"Hold on. I'm going to aim for the Sprite and Starburst." Ryan begins leading me over there, in a kind of ridiculous way, like we're doing a tango, pointing our hands toward the refreshment table.

I laugh. "We're going to get into trouble for taking the refreshments too early. Everyone will copy us. Chaos!"

"In D&D, I am aligned with chaotic good," he says modestly, twirling us closer and closer. He's getting the hang of it. "That means I'm kind, but I also do what I want."

"What am I?" I tilt my head back so I can see his expression.

He regards me thoughtfully. "Lawful good. That's the best kind. Honorable and compassionate. You fight evil and don't give up."

This makes me blush, for some reason. "I'm glad we're both good." I do try to be, I guess. Sometimes it's hard and maybe that's part of my problem. I'm always worried about being the best lawful good person I can be, even if I can't control it all. I shouldn't.

"Yeah," Ryan says. "You're actually the best lawful good ever."

"Why?" He seems like he's not joking for a change.

"Because you make me want to act better," he says seriously. "Because when I get onstage and I'm all amped up and too big, you bring me down."

"I bring you down? Gee, thanks."

"In a good way." He grins.

I think about this. "I guess . . . you help me be a little bit bigger, sometimes. We balance each other."

Ryan nods. "And because even though you're quiet, people listen to you when you do talk. Sometimes I feel like I talk so much that people miss it when I actually have a point." He blushes then, and I do, too, because we shared a lot. "So I guess what I'm trying to say, Ava, is you're pretty cool."

"Um." I don't want to leave that hanging in the air. "You're kind of cool, too."

Neither of us says anything for a minute. The lyrics go into the chorus, which are embarrassingly romantic. Why did Dad have to choose this song?

A memory of Dad telling Mom how she makes him a better person flits into my head. Ryan's not saying he's in love with me, is he? I stare hard at him, all squishy and weird inside.

"Anyway." Ryan bends his hip to the right. "Please excuse this awful thing I am about to do in advance." He screws up his face and he reminds me of Luke, and then even more so because Ryan lets out the stinkiest toot ever.

"Gross!" someone says.

I laugh because it's so disgusting and because I'm so relieved that Ryan is obviously not in love with me. Then Ryan lifts up my hand, and though Dad didn't teach us how to spin, he spins me anyway, and I follow like we've been doing it for years, and we dance away from the awful fart smell, laughing like crazy, and everyone in the auditorium's looking at us and wondering why we're having such a good time at Cotillion.

EPILOGUE

I don't see them in the sea of adult heads bobbing around. I turn and look behind me. What if they didn't come pick me up? I clutch my carry-on as I follow the airline lady down the escalator toward baggage claim, trying to spot them in the crowd. I really shouldn't have brought so many books and journals, but Zelia and I have a lot of catching up to do.

"Our claim is at B-2." The airline lady leads me over to the mass of people gathered around the machine. "You know what they look like, right?"

"Of course." I remind myself to relax. If Zelia and her mom aren't here, the airline will take care of me. I don't know how, but they will. Or I'll call my parents and they'll do something.

I will handle whatever happens.

I look around at the busy airport with all its shops, at the cars and buses honking outside, my insides a twisted knot of nerves and excited bunny hops. What is Maine going to be like? Zelia says we'll swim in a lake and go berry picking, two things I don't do in San Diego.

And then I spy a pink-and-blue head hopping up and down. "Ava!"

I run toward her, squirming my way through the adults. "Zelia!"

We hug. She's taller, but so am I, and we're seeing eye to eye for the first time in our lives, so that's different and a little odd. Shoulder to shoulder. Head to head. Her smile is just like I remember it, and the gleam in her eyes is the same.

"I have so much to show you!" she says, all sparkles and glitter, and then her mom appears with my Hello Kitty suitcase she's just picked up from baggage, and Zelia starts talking a mile a minute as we walk toward the doors.

I lean against her, happy to listen. Knowing now that when it's my turn, she'll listen to me.

The warm summer air hits me like a blanket, but it feels good after the closed-in air of the plane. I take a breath. "Ahhh. So this is Maine."

"Yeah. The airport is definitely the best part." Zelia puts her hands on her hips with her wry smile. "Well, you've seen it all. Might as well go home."

I turn around, pretending to leave.

"Oh my gosh. I've missed you so much." She grabs me and gives me another hug. "I'm so glad you made it!"

I'm glad I made it, too.

GAME:
FIVE THINGS

RULES:

Students stand in a circle.

One student starts by pointing at another and asking them to say five things as fast as they can based on a category of the initiator's choosing.

The student names five things. The things don't have to make sense. One of them could even be a noise. Every answer is correct.

As the student names each item, the rest of the class counts along, then cheers when five have been said. For example:

Initiator: Five things you'd find in a refrigerator.
Student: Milk!
Class: One!
Student: Orange juice!
Class: Two!
Student: A tree!

Class: Three!
Student: Ummmmm.
Class: Four!
Student: Mold!
Class: Five!

Now the entire class can sing a song/cheer as follows.

Entire class: (clapping with each word) These.
Are. Five. Things. (drawn-out) Fiiiive things.
(quickly) Five things. Five things. Five things.
These are five things!

The student who just named off five things will then point to another student and name a new category.

OBJECTIVES:
To revel in wordplay; to free your mind and commit to the moment; to support your teammates.

COMMENTS:
Encourage speed and not cleverness. Support the player with enthusiasm! Every idea is great. The point of improv is that "mistakes," the things that don't fit, are treasured.

Adapted from Canadian Improv Games.

GAME:
GIFTS

Two players face each other. Player A gives Player B an imaginary gift. You can play rounds of the best gift you can think of, the worst gift you can think of, the most boring gift, a gift that can fit in a shoebox, etc.

Player A says, "Here's a [blank]." Player B must answer, "Thank you, a [blank] is what I've always wanted! [Gives reason for wanting that gift.]" The reason can be absurd, it can be simple, or it can be a true reason. This game teaches the *yes, and* acceptance of unexpected things and how to build on what your partner gives you.

AUTHOR'S NOTE

There are two things I know run in my family: heart problems and anxiety. Like Ava, I was really anxious as a kid, which meant people thought I was shy. I often would refuse to talk at all, but made my ideas known through writing.

Like Ava, I also have noncompaction cardiomyopathy. It's genetic for me. My oldest brother and my mother and aunts died from it. The illness varies widely in severity. Some have spongy heart tissue and no symptoms, while others have hearts that get sick. So far I've been pretty lucky, but I have an ICD pacemaker implant in case the tissue decides to fail.

Though the causes vary, my cardiologist, Dr. Eric Adler at UCSD, who's also a researcher, said that it is thought that anxiety may cause the condition to surface. It became clear to me that I needed to find a way to control my anxiety and to teach my kids how to do so.

But despite therapy and mindfulness, controlling general and social anxiety was difficult. Until I took a long-form improv class in 2017. Long-form improv, unlike short form, is based more on relationships and situational comedy instead of thinking up comebacks or puns, and my writer brain loved it. It was like making up short plays.

I started taking classes because improv intrigued my creative side, and I thought it would help my writing (it does). To my great surprise I found it also helped my anxiety, and that it's actually used in some therapy settings, too. Like exposure therapy for anxiety, it gets you used to situations where you don't know what the outcome will be. It also helps with empathy and listening skills. Finally, it teaches you to not fear mistakes—because saying the wrong thing is the best part of improv.

And if you're doing it right, you support others as much as they support you. It's like a sports team that way, though I've never been on a sports team. If one of your teammates is flailing, you help out. You're never left hanging, either.

After seeing benefits for me, I had my thirteen-year-old daughter, who has the same brand of anxiety as I do, take improv twice. As time progressed, she began speaking up more in the classroom, even reading her own essay out loud to an auditorium full of people. She self-advocates expertly instead of remaining quiet. Most important, if she wants to participate in an activity, she's able to.

For these reasons and more, improv's also incredibly

beneficial for personal growth and interpersonal relationships. Room2Improv is a Chicago nonprofit that uses improv in schools to address bullying. Founder Eileen Kahana says that it helps bullies learn empathy and those who are bullied stand up for themselves. Many improv groups work with senior citizens and veterans' groups, too.

To further explore how improv can benefit you in your life, I suggest looking up improv theaters in your area and taking a class. Also check out the book *Relax, We're All Just Making This Stuff Up!: Using the Tools of Improvisation to Cultivate More Courage and Joy in Your Life* by Amy Lisewski.

ACKNOWLEDGMENTS

No book is created solo, and this book required more community participation than normal. When I began writing, I asked our community for input into improv and anxiety and/or introversion and how it helped them. I am so grateful to: Jay Sukow, an instructor and performer at Second City and other places; Amy Lisewski, owner of Finest City Improv and teacher; Jacqueline Bookstein, brilliant youth teacher and performer at Old Town Improv Company; Matt Sheelen and Ryan Suffridge of Cornerstone Improv; and Eileen Kahana of Room2Improv.

Improvisers that helped me with personal stories include Matt Messerman of National Comedy Theatre and Babel Barm of FCI. Hudson Reynolds, improviser extraordinaire at FCI and Old Town Improv Company, thoughtfully answered approximately a billion different technical questions with great patience and detail; I am grateful. Thanks also to my improv teachers at FCI: Tommy Galan, Shawn Roop, Joe Partynski, Amy Lisewski, and Jessica Farber; all of you influenced this book and helped me make these connections between improv and real life.

Shout-out to my improv team, Big Shoes, a group of people thrown randomly together by a class, who became good friends and teammates: JillAnne Aden, Mark Rachel, Diane Rachel, Tristan Cole, Randy Salgado, Mike Nieto, Stacey Willard, Melissa Slawson, Austin Beals, and Paul Wisecaver—you helped me understand what being on a real team is like. Big thanks to Collider Arts, where we're building something new and inclusive. To my sketch crew, which includes Gaby Reese, Tim Short, Ben Hardie, Mae Brayton, Damaris Treviso, Randy Salgado, and Stacey Willard—thanks for supporting my ideas and leadership with such enthusiasm—this helped inform the book more than you know. And finally to the whole FCI community—thanks for providing a space where background doesn't matter and where people can be their authentic selves.

Thanks to the ICD and noncompaction cardiomyopathy Facebook groups I belong to for providing me with their experiences, which helped inform Ava's. Thanks to my doctors at UCSD, Dr. Eric Adler and Dr. David Krummen, who have followed me closely and make sure I can do as many things as possible. Any factual mistakes about heart disease are my own.

I'm also extremely thankful for my critique group, Laura Shovan, Karina Yan Glaser, Casey Lyall, Timanda

Wertz, and Janet Sumner Johnson, who provided crucial early feedback. Thanks to my agent, Patricia Nelson, for her support and feedback. Thanks to Mary Pender at UTA for her continued support. My editor, Kristin Rens, brilliantly untangled and polished my story to be better than I had envisioned.

And, as always, thanks to my family for supporting and believing in me.